KRISTA'S
CHOICE

GEMMA
JACKSON

POOLBEG

Published 2020
by Poolbeg Press Ltd.
123 Grange Hill, Baldoyle,
Dublin 13, Ireland
Email: poolbeg@poolbeg.com

© Gemma Jackson 2020

The moral right of the author has been asserted.

A catalogue record for this book is available from the British Library.

ISBN 978178199-347-7

www.poolbeg.com

Also by Gemma Jackson

Through Streets Broad and Narrow

Ha'penny Chance

The Ha'penny Place

Ha'penny Schemes

Impossible Dream

Dare to Dream

Her Revolution

Published by Poolbeg

Foreword

Dear Reader,

Hello, thank you for following along. In *Krista's Choice* my young heroine finds employment as assistant to the mother of twin boys. What we would call an au-pair position. They do say write what you know.

I wanted to learn to speak foreign languages and knew there was no way my family could support me in my desire. The best way for me to succeed was to work for a family as an au-pair and study in the evening. To that end, I got a job with an artist in Brussels, Belgium.

What an adventure and blessing that turned out to be for me.

I was greeted at the airport by Grand-mère who had been educated in England. She was accompanied by Monsieur, and what a hunk of stuff he turned out to be – breathtaking. When we arrived at the four-storey house in the heart of Brussels, Madame was sunbathing in the garden – *NAKED!* When she came to greet me in the French way with a kiss on the cheek, I almost passed out. I was a holy Catholic girl from Ireland. I'd never even seen myself naked! We were taught your own body was an 'Occasion of Sin' and something to be shunned at all costs.

I had my own apartment in the house with en-suite and a balcony overlooking a tennis court where the famous tennis players of the day practised. Not that I was impressed. Well, I didn't know who they were.

All I can remember of the first weeks is the cry *"Non, Gemma, non!"*. I was told that after a week no English would be spoken. Well, I love to talk. I could make myself understood in French in no time. It might have been *"Me – you – go"* but it worked. I was soon chatting away in broken French.

I had cause to be grateful at times for my broken French. When Madame's dear friend and her fiancé came to lunch and showed photographs of their holiday at a nudist colony, I could blame my lack of French for my speechless state.

Sitting in that same garden years later, I told Madame of my impressions in those first weeks. We cried with laughter.

I was truly blessed with the family I lived with. There were four children – two boys, two girls. I took them to school and explored the area of Brussels on foot. I really was treated as a member of the family.

I like to get up and get out early. Madame and Monsieur, however, were slugabeds. I had to wait until I had tidied the kitchen before I could leave the house. So, I started serving them breakfast in bed which they thought was a wonder. I just wanted to get out of the house. In return, they served me breakfast in my apartment every Sunday morning.

I ran that house. In no time at all you had to ask Gemma's permission for everything!

Madame, a beautiful woman and a wonderful artist,

took me in hand and educated me in far more than French. I grew up under her careful guidance and counselling. Sitting in her garden on one of my many visits to her over the years, I told her how much she had inspired me. She was horrified. "My God!" she cried. "The responsibility, had I known I would never have dared open my mouth."

I arrived in Brussels in June so it was September before I could be enrolled for French lessons but, by that time, I spoke the language with ease. I was astonished by my fellow students. One Englishman had studied the language for sixteen years and couldn't form a sentence. I was at a disadvantage – when the teacher asked us to conjugate a verb the class lit up and shouted out in happy unison. I was lost but I could hold a conversation with the teacher.

It was a wonderful time. I learned so much about life and how to live it.

GEMMA

Chapter 1

"Abigail!" Violet Andrews stared at her friend. "Have you lost the run of your senses?" What on earth was she thinking of to blurt out a comment like that – and in the kitchen of all places? Yes, there had been talk of sending Krista on a mission into Germany but nothing had been decided and now was most definitely not the time to be talking about such things.

"I do not appreciate you glaring at me, Violet." Abigail, Lady Winchester, smiled around at the company. "I have become so fatigued with talks behind closed doors and discussions with bull-headed men. If we do not succeed in moving matters along, I fear I will be found babbling insensibly in a corner."

"Germany," Cordelia Caulfield – Lia to her friends

– gasped. "Would that not be rather dangerous at this time?" She couldn't imagine why her sister-in-law would want to send her youthful companion into Germany. Surely the girl had not long escaped from a perilous situation – why would anyone think of sending her back to the continent?

Peggy Matthews, the maid of all work at the Knightsbridge house, was, for once, keeping her mouth closed. Without being ordered, she began to remove the best tea service from the tray she'd prepared to carry upstairs – using them to set the wooden kitchen table. She couldn't wait to tell her mother that she'd been in the kitchen with a titled lady. Her mother would never believe it.

"Are you thinking of asking Krista to accompany the ladies travelling to Germany? The women planning to help remove children from that country are much older than Krista." Lia had become involved in raising funds for a group planning to remove German and Austrian children from what was rapidly becoming a danger zone.

Wilma Acers, the cook, set a heavy teapot on a silver trivet, covered the teapot with a knitted tea cosy and placed it on the table. She wished she could ask all of these people to get out of her kitchen. She had work to do. They could be chatting in any room in the house. Why they had chosen to park themselves in her little kingdom she did not know.

Krista sat in her employer's kitchen, listening to the company. Hadn't she been through enough changes already? She was in a strange country speaking a language not her mother tongue. She had left everything she had ever known behind in France and now they

2

wanted her to travel to Germany. She sometimes felt like a leaf in the breeze – blowing in all directions at the whim of the wind. The past four months had rocked and changed her world.

"The ladies moving the children are already in Germany," said Violet. "In my opinion it would be ill-advised to send Krista into Germany at this time. But I am afraid, ladies, we can no longer close our eyes to the fact that the world is changing around us." She accepted a cup of tea from Peggy. "I am afraid war is inevitable."

The old brigade from the WRNS had been writing to the War Office for months – and were mostly ignored. The women were becoming frustrated and threatening to set up their own groups – women who would be ready to step into the breach at the first moment of a threat to Great Britain.

"But – but – Prime Minister Chamberlin has assured us we will have peace. I heard him myself on the wireless." Wilma Acers felt she could say what she pleased in her own kitchen.

"Yes, indeed," Abigail sniffed.

She had been tempted in the last months to hit Neville Chamberlin around the head. She had never met a more stubborn man in her life and that was saying something. Since the arrival from France of her dear friend Violet Andrews in the company of young Krista and Herr Baron von Furstenberg, she had become involved in the world of politics. Her husband Albert, Lord Winchester, had been instrumental in introducing Herr Baron to men in power. Of course, she had not been included in these talks but Albert kept her informed and often asked her opinion.

"Mr Chamberlin believes every word out of Hitler's mouth," she said now. "I am afraid history will prove him mistaken."

"What has any of this to do with sending Krista to Germany?" Lia had agreed to employ Krista as companion and assistant only to appease her brother's wife. Abigail could be quite insistent when she wanted something done. She had grown to care for the girl in the months she had employed her and her twin sons David and Edward enjoyed her company.

"When war comes, and I am dreadfully afraid it will come," Violet said, "it will be the young who will be called to serve. Krista has skills that will make her valuable in the coming fight. You need to be made aware of this, Lia, as it will affect your household."

"My husband is a captain in the Royal Navy," Lia felt the need to remind them. "My household will be at the forefront of any sea battle."

"We know, my dear." Abigail covered Lia's clenched fist with her own soft hand. "Violet and I were Wrens in the last lot and proud to serve our navy in any way we could. We need to begin to train women to serve once more."

Abigail and Violet had been in talks with Dame Katherine Furse, the woman who quite literally wrote the book on how to set up the Women's Royal Naval Service after her experience in the Great War. The woman was a tower of strength and had essential information at her fingertips. She was being inundated with offers from ex-Wrens who wished to serve their country once more.

"The Admiralty, according to our sources," Violet said, "has been in endless talks and strategy meetings –

to no great effect as far as we can see. The ATS – the Auxiliary Territorial Service – have commenced recruiting volunteers in case of war. They have been given a brief to employ women as cooks, cleaners and waitresses to serve the forces. That is all very well in as far as things go but women will be needed in other roles and we of the old guard of the Wrens want to be ready to step into action." She stopped short of beating the tabletop but she was tempted. It was so frustrating trying to get the men from the admiralty to listen.

The women drank tea and talked of the work being carried out by groups of women around the country. They were trying to foresee the needs of the nation if or indeed when war was declared. It appeared a great number of people were working alone, trying to assist their continental cousins in any way they could. But these women agreed that Britain would be better served if women were called to serve and were organised by those with experience.

"I'll make a fresh pot of tea – that one must be stewed." Wilma, using a heavy wooden spoon, was beating sugar and butter together in a large porcelain bowl. The young lads were only in school for a half-day. She'd wanted to have something nice made for them when they returned home. She dropped the spoon into the bowl and wiped her hands on her apron with a sigh. It didn't look like she'd be getting this lot out of her kitchen any time soon.

"Peggy, be a dear and run fetch my cigarettes." Lia leaned back in her chair. "Krista, set the table up for a fresh pot of tea, please. Cook, do we have any cake? We may as well make ourselves comfortable."

"I need to use the WC." Abigail bustled out of the kitchen in the direction of the downstairs toilet.

"Smoking is really a filthy habit, Lia." Violet watched Krista remove the soiled dishes from the table and begin to set out a fresh tea set. "I am afraid we will all be indulging in the habit before too much longer – it is said to settle the nerves, don't you know? I believe I will use the WC too." She left the kitchen.

"Wilma, we are taking over your kitchen, I'm afraid." Lia looked at her cook, having been aware of Wilma's silent disapproval. But the large kitchen table with its wooden chairs really did make it more comfortable to sit around and talk. There were matters of importance to discuss and sitting back in comfortable chairs, while being attended by servants, simply did not give one the right atmosphere for discussing matters of importance – in her opinion. Besides, the table was out of the way to the side of the kitchen, allowing cook plenty of room to use her worktable and stovetop.

"It's your house Mrs Caulfield." Wilma was slicing a fruit cake. She'd make small sponge cakes for the lads. That didn't take much time to put together and bake. They preferred them anyway.

"There is a telephone call for Miss Andrews." Peggy came into the kitchen with cigarettes, lighter and ashtray in hand. "I let her know."

"Thank you, Peggy." Lia took the offered cigarettes and wasted no time in lighting one. "I didn't hear the phone ring."

"I was passing on my way to fetch your cigarettes and answered before it rang too many times." The phone sat proudly on a narrow table in the hallway.

"Who is Violet speaking to on the telephone?" Abigail returned to the kitchen, much refreshed.

Before anyone could answer, the kitchen door opened.

Violet almost exploded into the kitchen. "Ladies, you will not believe this!"

"What has happened?" Abigail grabbed her friend.

"That was Bettina Graham on the telephone," Violet gasped.

"*No!*" Abigail practically danced.

The other women in the kitchen watched the pair, wondering what in heaven's name could cause two mature women to behave like children – and in company.

"Bettina could not speak for long as she has many people to contact." Violet clasped her hands to her breast and seemed to need a moment to catch her breath. No one spoke. "The Admiralty has called upon a retired civil servant to work on a scheme to prepare a skeleton organisation and find principal female officers to take charge in case of emergency!"

"Not before time!" Abigail snapped. "But, my dear, a retired civil servant – what in heaven's name would the man know?"

"Well," Violet paused dramatically, "the first thing the man did was contact Dame Katherine Furse and ask for a consultation! They are in discussion even as we speak."

"A man of sense," Abigail sighed. "Finally."

"We must leave." Violet wanted to be in the thick of things. "The old girls are meeting at the Savoy Hotel to await developments."

Abigail clapped her hands, thrilled to think that – finally – matters were moving ahead. "Lia, thank you for your hospitality – we must away."

"Krista, there are matters we must discuss." Violet couldn't bear to be away from the action any longer. She had felt as if she were beating her head off a brick wall for months. "I will contact you and set up a date for a meeting." She almost ran to the kitchen door.

"Lia, you too may well be called upon to serve." Abigail followed Violet, with Lia on her heels.

"I have the children to consider," Lia was walking swiftly to keep up with her departing guests.

"My dear," Abigail turned on the doorstep to stare. "If what we have heard in recent months is true – London will not be safe for the children."

"Whatever do you mean?" Lia grabbed Abigail by the elbow, preventing her from leaving.

The car sat in the street, purring, with Violet gesticulating violently from the back seat.

"We will speak about this matter at a later date." Abigail pulled her arm free. "I simply must leave. I will telephone."

Lia stood open-mouthed in the doorway, watching the car speed away.

"Lia, if you will excuse me," Krista was at her employer's shoulder, "the children need to be collected from school."

Lia was jerked back to the present. "I will join you. David and Edward's first day at school. One cannot say it has not been memorable." She tucked the worry of what Abigail had said away, to think on later. Now she needed to collect her precious boys from school with a smile on her face.

The two women walked along the busy streets in silence, each lost in her own thoughts. Krista was still reeling from Lady Winchester's question about her willingness to travel to Germany. What on earth had that been about? It would be madness to return to the continent when she'd only just escaped the clutches of a violent man.

Lia fretted about the danger a possible war could pose for her sons. She'd become fixated with the danger her husband would face – but surely her boys would be safe? They were so young and innocent. Dear Lord, what would the future hold for all of them? Then she felt selfish. There were others in much worse circumstances than she.

They joined the crowd of servants and young mothers gathering before the gates of the school. A young woman was seen to open the double doors of the school wide – then jump swiftly out of the way. Children exploded from the dark interior of the school, skipping, shouting, laughing they poured towards the school gates, young eyes searching the waiting crowd.

"*Mama! Krista!*" David shouted. He had left the house that morning beautifully groomed, every hair in place. Now he looked like a disreputable lout. His knee-high grey stockings were in pleats towards his shoes, his shirt collar standing upright and buttons missing from his pale-blue shirt. The smile on his face stated that he'd enjoyed his first morning at school. The knees exposed by the gap between his socks and short grey trousers were caked with grime.

"Mama! Krista!" Edward walked over to them. His uniform was not quite as disreputable as his twin's, but it was obvious that he too had played roughly since they had been left at the school gates not that long ago.

"Do you see the boys anywhere, Krista?" Lea asked loudly, deliberately looking past the two ragamuffins standing in her path. "I can't see them."

"*Mama!*" David groaned.

"They must still be in school." Krista looked over the boys' heads towards the school doors.

"Mama, Krista, we are right in front of you!" Edward recognised this game and grinned.

"No, no, that cannot be." Lia played along. "I escorted two charming, gentlemanly boys, beautifully dressed, to school his morning – not two untidy brutes."

The twins laughed aloud, enjoying the game. They knew their mama would never be mad at them.

"I am hungry." Edward took his mother's hand. "We ate all of the food Cook gave us but I am still hungry."

"We have so much to tell you." David took his mother's free hand and one of Krista's.

With the boys walking alongside them, the women made their way home. The world might well be heading towards war but, at this moment in time, the women had two hungry little boys to feed.

Chapter 2

"Those two must have their teachers tearing at their hair." Perry laughed in open delight. He watched David and Edward scale a nearby tree, holding his breath until they had safely reached the first branch. "I now understand my nanny's despair at the constant untidy state of my clothing."

"The boys appear to have two speeds." Krista hurried to stand under the tree, her heart in her mouth in case one of the boys slipped. "Full speed ahead and full stop."

"They are fortunate to have you."

Perry had called in to the Knightsbridge house, hoping to tempt Krista into going for a walk in nearby Hyde Park. He knew the twins would accompany her but he enjoyed their company. It was a beautiful September

Saturday morning and he'd wanted to take advantage of the day in good company. The massage therapist his family had engaged to help strengthen his injured leg encouraged walking. He was now using a handsome silver-topped cane to get around.

"You allow them to be boys and run free. My own nanny, as far as I remember, appeared to be constantly yelling '*No!*' at the top of her lungs." He'd become quite the escape artist hiding from the nervous woman as often as was possible.

Krista smiled and accepted the implied compliment. No need to tell him she hadn't a clue what she was doing most of the time. She'd discovered running after the boys and preventing catastrophe was all she could manage on a day-to-day basis.

"They are showing *The Adventures of Robin Hood* at the Curzon cinema in Mayfair – would you care to accompany me this evening?" Perry held his breath. He had spent a great deal of time with Krista and the family she lived with but this was the first time he had invited her on an outing that could be considered a 'date' and he was nervous.

"Is that the film starring Errol Flynn?" Krista kept her eyes on the boys, not wanting Perry to see her delight. She had hoped he might be interested in asking her out on a date but, as the weeks passed, she had thought he'd seen her only as a friend. "I have heard of that film. They say it is a delightful romp."

"It is an American interpretation of a British story but I have heard it is frightfully amusing and the ladies seem to love Mr Flynn." Perry felt his heart beat faster. She was about to agree!

"I might have to arrange for someone to listen out for the boys." Krista didn't think that would be a problem. If Lia was going out or had company in, Peggy would be happy to help out. "I will ask Lia and, if she agrees, I would love to accompany you to the cinema." She felt quite breathless at the thought and was frantically doing a mental inventory of her wardrobe, wondering what to wear.

"*Krista!*" one of the boys shouted down from his perch in the tree. "*I'm hungry!*"

"*When are you not?*" Krista laughed. "*Come down then! I am not serving you up a tree!*"

The two boys scampered down with agile grace and landed with a thump on the leaf-covered ground.

"If you two gentlemen will find a bench that pleases you . . ." Krista had refused to allow Perry to carry her packed haversack. It was her job to look after the boys and she'd become accustomed to carrying emergency supplies on her back.

The two boys ran off, screaming their opinion of each bench they passed. Krista and Perry followed more slowly. The choosing of 'their' bench was becoming an important part of their days out. Krista was allowing the boys to run wilder than usual. The pair were finding sitting at a desk in school very difficult. They were not naughty children, just high-spirited.

When the bench had been chosen Krista removed her haversack and placed it on the wooden slats. She first removed the leather-cased knife she kept there, then allowed the boys to remove the items from the interior, standing smiling as they exclaimed over each item they removed. They'd had the same reaction as she'd packed the haversack.

Perry had used the back of the heavy bench cemented into the pathway to lower himself to the grass. He sat with his injured left leg stretched out, trying not to groan in relief. He dropped the cane to his side, pulled his right leg up and wrapped his arms around his knee, content to sit and watch the little drama being played out in front of him. He was so grateful to Krista for including him in her day-to-day life. He had been bored with his own company when he met her.

Krista removed the leather cover from the knife and pushed the cover into her slacks pocket. She used the knife to slice a firm green apple in half, offering each boy a half. She turned with a smile to Perry. "Would you care for an apple, Perry?"

"Thank you." He took the apple from her hand, flashing his dimples. "Is that not what Eve said to Adam?"

"I've always thought that was just an excuse to blame women for the worries of the world." Krista was aware of the boys taking in their every word. She turned to them. "Who wants lemonade?" The flask she carried had two metal cups that served as a top to the flask and were ideal for serving drinks to two active boys.

"*Me!*" David shouted.

"*Me!*" Edward's voice came at almost the exact moment as his twin's.

She served the boys the drinks and sandwiches, very conscious of Perry watching her.

Perry bit into the apple, surprised by its sharp tangy taste. He would have thought Edward and David would prefer something sweeter. He watched Krista deal with her charges, fascinated anew by this woman

14

who dared to leave everything she knew to travel to England. He'd never met anyone like her. Look at her in her slacks – so daring! She seemed unaware of the glances she was receiving from the passing crowd – not everyone approved of women wearing slacks, but he thought she looked delightful.

"This apple is delicious," he said.

"It's called a Granny Smith," David wanted to be the first to name the apple.

"Don't speak with your mouth full, David." Krista had taken a seat between the two boys, hoping to fend off spillages and the push-pull action the twins sometimes indulged in.

"An old woman in Australia discovered the apples. That's why they are called Granny Smiths." Edward had hastily swallowed his bite of sandwich so he could be the one to tell what he knew. "The woman had emigrated to Australia from England." He puffed out his chest, thrilled he knew something Perry might not.

"Is that a fact?" Perry knew the story of the discovery of the Granny Smith apple but enjoyed the boy's interpretation of the story which was used extensively in promoting the apples.

"The woman spit the apple pits out of her kitchen window and a tree grew." David had cleared his mouth to join the conversation.

The two adults sat and were entertained by the boy's interpretation of the story Krista had told them. She found that the boys were interested in the world around them. She tried to keep their interest engaged by telling them stories that would appeal to them.

"Krista, look!" Edward, his sandwich consumed,

pointed towards a man nearby, lying on his opened newspaper spread on the grass. "*Can we do that?*" His whisper was loud.

"Don't point." Krista drew his little hand down. "It is not polite."

"But can we?" David urged.

Perry waited for Krista to correct David's grammar. When she remained silent, he laughed under his breath. English was not Krista's native tongue after all. How many times had he been told the difference between 'may I' and 'can I'? The lesson was usually accompanied by a clip around the ear.

Krista removed a towel from the bottom of the haversack. It wasn't very large but the boys should fit on it.

"The towel is too narrow for you to lie side by side. You can lie top to tail," She told them, shaking out the white towel. Peggy had told her of her family's need to sleep 'top to tail'. "You will need to remove your shoes."

She put the towel on the grass close to where Perry sat. The boys giggled with excitement, thrilled to be allowed to lie down outdoors. It took them a few moments to work out the logistics of lying so close together. They had to be cautioned not to put their feet in each other's face but they soon settled down.

"That didn't take long," Perry said softly after a while.

The boys were breathing deeply, each falling asleep after their morning of activity.

"I didn't think it would." Krista was repacking the haversack, making sure she had everything she had brought with her. The towel could be pushed on top and taken out when they returned home to be washed.

16

When her haversack was packed and closed, she threw it on the grass and sat down to join Perry, glad once more for her slacks. She pulled her knees up to her chest and crossed her arms around them, staring over at the children.

"What have you heard about the people taking the children from the continent?" Perry had become involved with the women fundraising and planning the journey to remove children at risk from Germany and Austria.

"Lia informed me that the ladies have arrived at the places that have been chosen as starting points. That is all that is known at the moment." Krista worried and wondered about those women sent to guide the children across countries and the sea. "It will not be an easy task."

"Do you believe we are heading for war?" Perry glanced at his left leg with an expression of disgust, once more cursing the riding accident that had left him in this helpless state. He would already have joined the service if he'd been fit for action.

"*Shhh!*" Krista carefully observed the twins. They sometimes pretended to be asleep and listened to what was being discussed around them. "They are asleep." She rested her head on her bent knees, staring at Perry. She was aware of his frustration with the limitations his injury put on his life. "I am no expert, Perry, but I believe that war is coming. Whether Great Britain will be involved in that war I do not know. However, my guardian Miss Andrews and her closest acquaintances from the women who served in the Women's Royal Naval Service are convinced that we will be at war in the near future."

"My own mother is an ex-Wren – have I mentioned that before?" Perry asked.

17

"No, you have not." Krista had not met Perry's family. He didn't speak a great deal about his home life. They did not speak of their family when they met. Krista had no wish to discuss her time spent with the Dumas family in France. She had been reluctant to open that topic of conversation. When they met, they discussed their own hopes and plans for the future.

"Yes, indeed." Perry was at a loss to know how to act around Krista. She was not one of the groomed debutantes that his parents insisted on introducing him to. Would they approve of her? Did he care? "My mother is a great deal younger than my father." His father had been a widower with children almost the same age as she when they met. "They actually met when she was serving in the Wrens during the Great War." He had never told Krista his full family name or that his father was an admiral.

"I wonder if Miss Andrews knows your mother?" Krista, from listening to Miss Andrews and Lady Winchester discuss their time in the Wrens, had begun to believe it had been one big happy family with everyone knowing everyone else. But that surely couldn't be true?

"It would be beyond strange if she did. There were a great many women serving in the Navy during the Great War." Perry hadn't ever thought of Krista's guardian knowing his parents. He should have.

"Have you thought about what you will do if Great Britain joins the war?" Krista almost held her breath. They avoided discussing Perry's limitations but she felt time was running out and they could no longer avoid the subject.

"I thought I should take up knitting socks for the troops." Perry allowed his bitterness to show. "I have been informed – repeatedly – that my leg will not stand up to active duty. I would be a liability." He threw himself back on the grass and covered his eyes with his bent arm.

Krista felt sad for her friend. She had seen over the last weeks that he sometimes became very disheartened. But there was no time to feel sorry for oneself. Perry had much to offer if he could only be made to see that.

"Well, Mr Carter, you may lie there and proclaim your woes to the sky," Krista refused to allow her sympathy to show. "Or you can take your own fate in your hands and do something."

"What would you suggest?" Perry removed his arm from his eyes to glare up at the beauty by his side.

"You have received a good education, have you not?" This too was something they hadn't discussed but it was obvious to anyone with eyes that Perry was not a member of the working class.

"My parents insisted upon it." He was sulking and knew it.

"Perry," Krista reached out one hand and shook him slightly, "you need to think about what you have to offer. There is more to war than shooting a gun. The men will have to have supplies, plans will have to be drawn up." She threw her hands in the air. "Oh, I don't know. I am not a general. What do I know of war? But what I do know is that you need to find out what is needed and where you might help. There is a job somewhere that only you can do. Find it."

"You are quite the little spitfire, are you not?" Perry

sat up, feeling cheered by her words. She was correct – he wasn't useless – he surely had a lot to offer – if he could only figure out what.

"*Krista, I'm thirsty!*" David's sleepy voice called.

"*I need to go to the toilet!*" Edward added.

"It looks like our private time is over." Perry was relieved at the interruption.

"They don't nap for long but wake refreshed." Krista pushed to her feet, wiping off the seat of her slacks with her hands.

"Come with me, young man." Perry once more used the back of the bench, this time to pull himself upright. He held out his hand to Edward, intending to lead him to a nearby tree. There was no need to rush home to use the toilet. Nature wouldn't mind if the twins used her bounty.

Krista laughed and stood watching as Perry, followed by the two little men, walked towards the nearest tree. It would appear the twins were going to get a lesson in how to urinate outdoors.

Chapter 3

"How do I look?" Krista stood in the kitchen with her arms spread, turning slowly for Peggy's inspection. The dress she was wearing was floral-print white cotton, buttoned to the waist, with half sleeves and a full skirt that fell past her knees. Her legs gleamed in silk stockings.

The boys were in bed. Mrs Acers had returned to her own home. The girls had the kitchen to themselves.

"I'd almost forgotten you had legs." Peggy laughed. "You wear those slacks so much."

"But what do you think of the dress?" Krista was so nervous. This was her very first date and she wanted to make a good impression.

"I don't know what you're worried about. Honest

to goodness, everything you wear is gorgeous. I can't believe how everything matches everything else. I couldn't do that if my life depended on it."

Peggy envied her friend. Imagine going to one of them posh picture houses in Mayfair. She was lucky if she got invited to the fleapit close to her family home. She'd be in the back row of the picture house, fighting for her virtue. That wouldn't happen to Krista. There was just something about the girl that screamed class.

"Emmanuelle Doumer, Her Ladyship's maid, picked all of my clothes." Krista ran her hand lovingly down the dress.

"Look at how the blue in those flowers matches the blue of your T-strap shoes!" Peggy wondered what it would be like to wear clothes like that. She stifled a sigh. She'd never know. "Are you going to wear your lovely blue coat?"

"It is not that cold. I thought I would wear my blue cardigan over the dress. I don't want to look overdressed." Krista was wondering how they would get to the picture house. He couldn't walk the mile-long distance from Knightsbridge to Mayfair with his damaged leg.

"May I join in this conversation?" Lia was standing just inside the kitchen doorway. The two girls had been so involved in their discussion they hadn't noticed her. How different this was from her own first outing with a young man, she thought. The hours and days of discussion about her gown, the jewels she should wear! The young man had been stiff with fear and she hadn't been much better. Ah well, long ago and far away. She walked into the kitchen and put the kettle on, simply for something to do with her hands. The two young girls were standing as if frozen.

"I can do that!" Peggy grimaced at Krista – sometimes this being friendly with the mistress of the house could be awkward.

"It's done now." Lia shrugged.

"What do you think, Lia?" Krista once more turned in a slow circle. "Will this do for a visit to the picture house?"

"You look charming." Lia stepped closer. "I like what you have done with your hair. Are you wearing cosmetics?"

"Just a touch." Krista held still while she was examined. "Her Ladyship's maid showed me how to darken my lashes and eyebrows and to use a little rouge."

"Emmanuelle – the woman is a wonder." Lia admired the soft touch of colour and how it brightened Krista's face.

"I think she should wear her blue coat and the hat and gloves she wore when she arrived here." Peggy said. "She looked ever so glamorous."

"Won't that be a little overdressed for a visit to a picture house?" Krista asked.

"Perry is taking you to the Curzon in Mayfair?" Lia waited for Krista's nod before continuing. "It is a very beautiful theatre and I doubt very much you will be seated in the cheap seats." She laughed and tried to suppress the image of Krista and Perry down in front of the screen, craning their necks to see Robin Hood swing from the greenery. Krista may not have realised Perry's family were wealthy and from the upper echelon of British society but Lia knew. She was a member of that society. "You should wear your coat and whatnot – the evenings are closing in and becoming chilly. You may leave your outer garments in the Curzon cloakroom."

"Did you want tea or coffee, Mrs Caulfield?" Peggy was holding the steaming kettle aloft, waiting to see what she needed to do next.

"I think a pot of camomile tea, please, Peggy. It will soothe the nerves." Lia had completely forgotten she'd put the kettle on to boil.

"I don't want to embarrass Perry." Krista didn't want tea. She wanted help and advice. "He can't walk very far without suffering. I don't want to be all dressed up if we are taking the bus to Mayfair."

Lia couldn't help it. The sound of her laughter echoed around the kitchen. The two mystified young girls staring at her just made her laugh more. Imagine, Peregrine Fotheringham-Carter taking his date on the bus! It was too funny.

"You see, Lia," Krista stood with her hands on her hips, "even you think it's comic."

"I have no doubt Perry has ordered a taxi to carry you to the theatre." Lia had to force herself to stop laughing.

"Run up and put your coat and hat on." Peggy was putting the white flowered teapot they kept for floral teas on the table. She had already set out cups and saucers and the bee-decorated honey jar. "You can model it for us."

"I'll be right down." Krista hurried from the kitchen.

"She seems very nervous." Lia sat at the kitchen table, reaching for the teapot.

"It's her first time going out with a young man." Peggy joined her mistress when Lia gestured to a chair across the table from her.

"But she and Perry have been together so often this summer." Lia herself had never spent so much time in the company of a young man without adult supervision.

"This is different." Peggy used the spiral spoon from the honeypot to add a large dollop of honey to her tea. She didn't like fancy light flowery tea but she'd put up with it.

"Is it? How?" Lia sipped her tea without honey.

"Krista and Perry have been running around as mates this summer." Peggy didn't know how the mistress couldn't see the difference but she'd try to explain. "They've been friends having a laugh and a joke together – keeping each other company." She paused for a moment to think. "Tonight is different. Perry has changed the rules on her. He asked her out on a date. I know she was hoping he'd ask her but, now that he has, she is not too sure how she feels about it."

"I see," Lia said doubtfully.

"No, you don't at all." Peggy laughed. "They were being kids together this summer but tonight is adult. Do you see?"

The doorbell rang before Lia could answer. Peggy pushed to her feet.

"Blimey, he's eager!" She muttered on her way out of the kitchen to answer the doorbell.

Lia couldn't resist following and climbing the stairs to quietly stand and watch the happenings in the long hallway.

"Well, well, aren't you a sight for sore eyes!"

Lia couldn't see who was at the door as Peggy was blocking her view.

"You look very handsome this evening." Peggy had

25

almost swallowed her tongue when she opened the door. He looked like a film star. That suit he was wearing never came off the thirty-bob rail at a gents' outfitters. That was Savile Row or she'd eat her hat. If she was wearing one, like.

"Evening, Peggy." He doffed his grey Trilby hat which matched his suit exactly. He had come to know Peggy Matthews over his visits to this house and enjoyed her irreverence. "I have a taxi waiting – is Krista ready?"

"Step in a minute," she said.

Lia almost clapped her hands from where she'd stepped into the shadows at the foot of the hall. She'd wanted a good look at him in all his glory.

Peggy walked to the bottom of the stairs. "*Krista!*" She slapped her open hand to her forehead. "Oh! I forgot the boys are asleep!"

"I heard the doorbell, Peggy!" Krista came running lightly down the stairs.

Peggy stepped back as Perry walked to the bottom of the stairs and stared.

"You look delightful." He smiled, flashing his dimples, causing all three women to sigh.

"Thank you, kind sir!" Krista was having difficulty taking in the glory that was Perry. She had never seen him so formally dressed. He was stunning.

"Shall we go?" He offered his arm, his white-knuckled grip on the head of his cane the only outward sign of his own nerves.

Lia waited until Peggy had closed the door after the couple.

"Peggy, I intend to spend this evening writing letters.

There is no need for you to remain. Why don't you visit your family?"

"Oh, missus, thank you! I'd love that."

Peggy ran to change.

Lia went upstairs to stand at the window looking down at the entrance to her home. She would wait until Peggy left before placing a telephone call to her sister-in-law, Lady Abigail. The position of the telephone in the main hallway of the house could sometimes result in servants hearing more than one was comfortable with.

"Abigail," Lia was standing in the hallway, the phone receiver pressed to her ear. She had one ear open for the boys. They seemed to have an unnatural ability to hear whatever one wanted to keep from them. They delighted in pretending to be asleep. She had no intention of discussing this situation in depth. One knew the telephone operators listened in to telephone calls. It was against company policy, of course, but one knew not to discuss delicate matters openly on the telephone. "I have had a great deal of difficulty reaching you."

"Oh, my dear," Abigail's voice came sweetly over the telephone line, "I have become a social butterfly. I do not know from one moment to the next where I will be myself." Abigail had to clench her teeth not to allow her frustration to escape. She and her fellow ex-WRN's had been sent thither and yon for days. If something were not done soon, she would be responsible for physically harming some of the dullards commanding the navy, each one more afraid to take an actual decision than the other.

"I telephoned in the hope of arranging a meeting

with you – you and Violet Andrews – as soon as might be possible." Lia needed to speak to the two women face to face.

"My dear –"

"Oh, before I forget to mention," Lia interrupted before Abigail could refuse. "Our dear Krista had her first date with a young gentleman this evening. The pair looked quite delightful as they left here. I was quite overcome. You could almost touch the emotion they share for each other." She took a deep breath. "Yes, indeed, dear Krista and her escort Peregrine Fotheringham-Carter looked like film stars as they stepped out together this evening."

A gasp echoed down the telephone line. There was silence for a moment.

"Yes, young love!" Lia said into the shocked silence. "Such a thrill to witness it."

"We must get together." Abigail understood the urgency. "I will consult Violet and we will arrange a rendezvous."

"I will wait to hear from you." Lia put down the receiver without saying goodnight.

There was no need. Both women understood that the budding romance between Perry and Krista must be stopped. The Fotheringham-Carters would never allow a son of theirs to become involved with a socially unacceptable woman. There could be no happy outcome from the relationship. Lia would not stand back and watch Krista enter a relationship that would lead to tears and heartbreak.

Lia sighed deeply. She could do nothing about Krista at this moment. She would write to Charles and her many friends this evening, keeping the letters light-hearted. There was no need to involve Charles in domestic worries. She would write an amusing letter, enjoying the image of his smile.

While others worried about her, Krista was trying desperately not to appear a country bumpkin. The picture house Perry took her to was one of the most glamorous buildings she had ever been inside. In the past she had been fortunate if the local gathering hall in Metz showed a film. Everyone sat on hard wooden benches with their coats and whatnot on their laps. Here, it was an edifice. There was a cloakroom with a uniformed lady to take your outer wear. The carpet underfoot was lush and deep. She was turning her head – she hoped discreetly – to try and take everything in. Peggy would want to hear all about this evening.

They were seated in the first row of the balcony in wide deep velvet-covered seats. The open area in front of their seats allowed Perry to stretch out his injured leg.

Errol Flynn, the actor portraying Robin Hood, looking very manly in his green tights, swung through the greenery. Olivia de Haviland as Maid Marian tore at the heartstrings. As for that fiend, the Sheriff of Nottingham, marvellously portrayed by Basil Rathbone – a British actor – Krista had joined the audience in hissing in disapproval when he appeared on screen.

She'd been forced to elbow Perry a number of times in the ribs when he'd started snorting at the American interpretation of Britain's fictional hero. She was perfectly willing to accept everything she was seeing on screen.

Dear Perry had purchased a beautiful box of Cadbury

Milk Tray chocolates for her – an entire box! She hadn't opened the box, too enthralled by the action playing out on the screen in front of her.

Perry was sitting back in his seat, enjoying Krista's reaction to everything far more than the action playing out on the screen. A man swinging through the trees, wearing green tights with a feather in his cap! It was too ridiculous for words. He was enjoying teasing Krista and her elbow had made contact with his ribs several times already. She was so enthralled with the action on screen that she had not even opened the box of chocolates he'd purchased for her. What a girl! Time spent with her had saved his sanity. She was not a girl who would allow him to wallow in self-pity.

"What has happened?"

Krista's dismay took him from his own thoughts. He glanced at the screen and laughed.

"It is the interval, my dear." At his words the lights in the cinema came up, the doors to the side of the rows of seating opened and young women with large trays at their waists began to form a line around the walls of the picture house. The trays offered frozen delights, cigarettes, matches and anything the film crowd might enjoy.

"Would you care for some ice cream?"

"I'd love one! But, Perry, where are those people going?" Krista saw that a great number of people were leaving their seats. "The film is not over."

"There is a bar open for the enjoyment of those who wish a drink," Perry said, "and some would be taking the chance to visit the facilities."

"Oh Perry!" Krista's smile was so wide it almost hurt her face. "Isn't this wonderful?"

Chapter 4

OCTOBER 1938
Knightsbridge

Lia and Krista had just returned from leaving David and Edward to school. They had enjoyed a leisurely stroll back to the house, making plans for the day ahead.

Lia looked at the Rolls Royce sitting, its engine idling, in front of her house. "Isn't that Abigail's car? She must be waiting for me inside."

They hurried up to the front door. As they did so, it swung open, revealing Abigail standing inside, looking distraught.

"Good heavens, Abigail, whatever is the matter?"

"There is no time for pleasantries." Abigail grabbed at Krista's arm, pulling her through the open doorway. "Quickly, upstairs, Peggy is waiting for you." She waited for Lia to step into the hallway and slammed the door closed.

"What is happening?" Lia watched Krista run up the stairs.

"*Why will men not listen to women?*" Abigail threw her arms in the air. "I was forced to almost physically stop Violet from accompanying me here today. She is incandescent with rage and would only have made matters worse."

"Abigail, what is happening?"

"There is no time for deep discussion." Abigail wanted to lie down in a dark room and scream. "The Metropolitan Police have issued a warrant for Krista's arrest. A car has been dispatched and is on its way here even as we speak."

"Abigail, what have you got me involved in?" Lia had been trying to speak privately with Abigail for weeks about Krista's growing friendship with Perry. The woman had been avoiding her. Now this!

"Come!" Abigail practically towed Lia towards her own drawing room. "We must not be caught standing in the hallway." She crossed her fingers, praying that Krista had enough time to change her clothing – one's appearance could quite set the tone. It was important that Krista look like a well-brought-up young woman – not a hellion in slacks!

"*Abigail!*"

"It is the fault of men who refuse to listen to women who know more about a situation than they do." Abigail was listening for the sound of a car stopping in the street.

Krista ran into her bedroom to find Peggy had spread out her best clothes on the bed. The other girl was practically bouncing in place.

"Peggy, do you know what is happening?"

"Her Ladyship sent me up here to get your clothes ready." Peggy was pulling at Krista's clothing as she spoke. "She wants you out of those slacks and into your best outfit as quickly as possible. I've polished your shoes and freshened your hat and gloves. Quick," she pulled at Krista, trying to get her to move, "you have to get changed."

"Why?"

"You don't ask Her Ladyship why – you just jump to obey. I would have thought you knew that already." Peggy pulled each item of clothing away as Krista removed them. When the other girl didn't move fast enough for her she began pulling the slip and underskirt over her head herself.

"I have to get back downstairs," Peggy said when Krista was dressed. "You do your own hair and face. Her Ladyship wants you looking like you just stepped off the cover of a magazine." She turned to run from the room, fizzing with excitement.

The ringing of the doorbell as Peggy reached the last few stairs nearly caused her to trip. She reached the black-and-white tiles of the hall and took a moment to breathe deeply before walking over to open the door. She almost disgraced herself by gasping when she saw the uniformed policeman standing in the open door. A police car was in the street behind Her Ladyship's Rolls Royce, a second policeman behind the wheel.

"Is your mistress at home?" Sergeant Ted Black didn't know why he and his partner had been sent to pick up a young woman from what appeared to him to be a respectable house. That Rolls Royce and chauffeur out there cost a pretty penny to run.

"Yes, sir." Peggy didn't know how to behave. She had never opened the door to a policeman before.

"If I could have a moment of her time?"

"I will inform Mrs Caulfield that you wish to speak with her." Peggy left the door open but she wasn't going to invite him inside. Without waiting for his response, she walked swiftly into the drawing room. She was glad she'd heard Her Ladyship's voice coming from that room or she would have been forced to search the house for her mistress – so undignified.

"There is a policeman here to see you, Mrs Caulfield." Peggy was speaking almost before she crossed the threshold into the room.

"A policeman?" Lia glared at Abigail who still hadn't told her what was going on – she said it was too complicated to explain in a hurry. "Show him in." What else could she do or say?

Peggy returned to the front door.

"If you will follow me, please, sir." Peggy waited for the man to step inside and closed the door. She led the way into the drawing room and the two waiting women.

"Mrs Caulfield." Ted Black removed his hat and held it on one bent arm.

"I am Mrs Caulfield," Lia said. She waved her arm towards her companion, "My sister-in-law Lady Winchester. How may we help the Metropolitan Police?"

"Mrs Caulfield, Your Ladyship." Ted Black wanted to curse. A titled woman. That was all he needed. "Mrs Caulfield, you have a young foreign woman working for you, I believe."

"Yes, my assistant Krista is French."

"I have been sent to escort her to New Scotland Yard." That was all he knew. "She is wanted for questioning."

"I beg your pardon!" Lia's words covered Peggy's gasp.

"What nonsense!" barked Her Ladyship. "Krista and I have planned a morning shopping."

"I am sorry, ladies." Ted Black straightened his spine. "I have my orders."

"Peggy, ask Krista to come down, please," Lia said.

"I will accompany Krista," her ladyship stated.

"I am sorry, Your Ladyship. That isn't possible. I was told only to take the young lady into my custody and deliver her to New Scotland Yard." Ted Black would obey his orders and allow someone else to cross swords with the titled woman.

The three people waited in silence.

"Peggy said there is a problem?" Krista walked into the drawing room wearing her best outfit, her hair gleaming under her white hat, handbag under her arm and white leather gloves held in one fist.

"Krista, my dear, you look delightful." Abigail jumped to her feet before anyone else could speak. "I am afraid our morning of shopping must be postponed. This policeman has been sent to escort you to New Scotland Yard. It is the home of the Metropolitan Police." She was unsure if the girl would recognise the address of police headquarters. "I am sure it is a mistake. Unfortunately, they refuse to allow me to accompany you."

Ted Black almost swallowed his tongue when the stunning beauty turned terrified blue eyes in his direction.

"Are you sure you have the right person?" Krista

had almost vomited when Peggy told her the police were downstairs looking for her.

"I am sorry, miss. There is no mistake. I was given your name and this address."

"I am sure this is some sort of misunderstanding, Krista." Lia couldn't refuse to allow Krista to be removed by the police. "Do you have enough cash on you to pay for a taxi when this matter has been sorted out?"

"Thank you. I do." Krista had to lock her knees to remain standing.

"If you would come with me, miss." Ted Black gave a brisk nod of the head to the two ladies. "Thank you, Mrs Caulfield, Your Ladyship."

"Peggy, see the officer out." Lia was trying desperately hard not to glare at her sister-in-law. That woman knew more than she was telling. She waited until she heard the closing of the front door before stepping into the hall. "You can join Mrs Acers in the kitchen, Peggy."

"Yes, Mrs Caulfield. Should I ask Cook to send up a tea tray?"

"Thank you, no, Peggy." Lia needed something a great deal stronger than tea. She reached out to grab on to Abigail's arm as the woman tried to move around her to exit the room. "You are going nowhere until you tell me what on earth is going on!"

"I merely wish to send my car away."

"See that you come straight back, Abigail, or I will make a show of myself running after your car screaming." Lia felt capable of carrying out her threat. "I am going to pour myself a large whiskey, would you care for one?"

"Yes, please." Abigail was opening the door as she spoke. "This morning has quite shredded my nerves."

"Now, Abigail, tell all." The two women were sitting in the family room, large glasses of whiskey in hand.

"I don't know if I know all." Abigail sipped her drink, feeling exhausted, and it wasn't even midday.

"Don't dance around the subject!" Lia snapped. "I have been trying to speak with you about Krista for weeks. I have told you she is becoming romantically linked with Peregrine Fotheringham-Carter. I have asked repeatedly to meet with you and you have fobbed me off." She threw her hands in the air, almost spilling her drink. "Then this morning ..." She stopped.

"I really don't know everything," Abigail pinched the bridge of her nose, hoping to release some of the pressure in her head. She held up one hand when Lia went to speak. "A friend of Bertie's," she used her husband's family pet name, "telephoned last evening to discuss an idea or is it a plan – I really don't know nor do I care."

"You are rambling, Abigail."

"I know you were shocked when I mentioned the possibility of Krista travelling to Germany."

"Abigail, would you get on with it, please, or the boys will be home from school before you have told me the story."

"The government has begun making a listing of all those with knowledge of a foreign language. There is a desperate need for young people who can speak foreign languages fluently. Krista's name has been mentioned on many occasions. She does speak three languages fluently after all."

"What has that got to do with the police turning up on my doorstep?"

"The powers that be, in their wisdom want to interrogate Krista." She ignored Lia's gasp. "They wish to establish that Krista is not a foreign spy."

"How utterly ridiculous!" Lia said in disgust.

"Men!"

"But there is more to Krista than meets the eye." Lia wasn't going to let Abigail off the hook. "I knew that from the first moment you asked me to offer her a home."

"Yes, indeed." Abigail stood and walked over to the long window overlooking the small garden to the rear of the house. She placed her glass on the windowsill and crossed her arms. She leaned against the window frame, looking out with unseeing eyes. "Krista, that poor dear child."

Lia walked across the room to take up position across the window frame from Abigail.

"I don't know if you remember my friend Lady Constance ..." Abigail said.

"Stowe-Grenville," Lia gasped. "Of course I remember her. She was quite the most dashing woman I had ever met in my life."

"You were very young when the scandal broke." Abigail never took her eyes from the miserable little garden. It was more a yard really, she thought absently. "What would you have been – ten or eleven years old? Still in the schoolroom."

"I was fifteen when Lady Constance was killed – somewhere on the continent, wasn't it?" Lia was trying to recall the details of that time. "I was saddened to hear of her death. You can have no idea of the effect you, Lady Constance and Violet Andrews had on an impressionable young girl. You were all so full of life and laughter. It was watching you three that made me determine to live my life to my own rules."

"Really?" Abigail shook her head. "I never knew."

"You entered my life like a cyclone." Lia hated to see Abigail's eyes dull with sorrow. She was everything light and fun. "I watched you and Bertie together, delighted to know that something more than icy politeness was possible between husband and wife."

"Your parents ..." Abigail left it at that. The pair had almost given her frostbite. She had locked horns with them from the very first meeting.

"You entered that house with your friends and new ideas, shaking up all of the old rules." Lia laughed. "It was because of you that I was sent away to school. My parents were terrified you would infect their youngest child." She bobbed a curtsey. "I thank you for that."

"Dear Lord," Abigail sighed. "It seems so long ago and far away ..."

"But, Abigail . . . what has all of this to do with Krista?"

"Krista –" Abigail bit back a sob – she couldn't allow herself to become maudlin. "Krista is the daughter of Lady Constance."

"No!" Lia tried frantically to think of anything she might have heard at the time of Lady Constance's death but it was so long ago and life had moved on.

"Yes, indeed. Krista was in the car with Constance and her paramour when the accident happened. She has no idea – no idea at all."

Lia didn't know what to say.

"You were concerned because Krista was stepping out with Peregrine Fotheringham-Carter. My dear, Krista's blood is much bluer than his, I assure you."

"But she is baseborn." Lia knew how the landed gentry saw such things.

"So were the ancestors of more than half the royal households of Europe!" Abigail snapped.

"Not everyone thinks as daringly as you." Lia almost laughed. Even after all of these years as a titled lady, Abigail still walked her own path.

"Violet and I have opened a can of worms, I'm afraid." Abigail resisted the urge to pick up the crystal glass and fling it across the room. She was more than angry – deep inside she was frightened. "We approached an old friend of ours, seeking papers for Krista. She doesn't have any, as you know. That situation can't continue. We want her to become legally established in England." If only Anthony Eden was still in the Foreign Office but the man had retired his position earlier in the year because of Chamberlain's pandering to Hitler.

"But why have the police become involved? Krista is not a criminal."

"Krista is not being interrogated by the police as a criminal." Abigail leaned her head against the cool window pane. "She has been summoned to meet with some wallah from the SIS."

"The Secret Intelligence Service." Lia felt sick to her stomach. How would something of this nature affect her husband's career?

"They want to send Krista into Germany as a spy – have you ever heard anything so ridiculous?"

Both women stood staring at nothing in particular,

each wondering where Krista was and what she was being subjected to.

"Is there nothing we can do to help?" Lia might worry about her husband's career, but she would not see the girl forced to risk her life because it appeared she had no family to protect her.

"All we can do is wait and pray." Abigail turned from the window. "I'll have that pot of tea now, Lia."

Chapter 5

Krista sat in the back of the police car, a silent policeman at her side. She fought tears as the car passed Buckingham Palace. She'd walked past that building almost daily with the twins. Her stomach fluttered with fear but she remained silent, wondering what awaited her at the police station. What had she done to bring the police to her employer's door?

"Take the rear entrance," the police sergeant leaned forward to say to the driver.

The car passed before the red-brick building that housed the head office of the Metropolitan Police. The driver turned down the covered tunnel that opened between two buildings and drove into a stable yard. Men and horses seemed to be everywhere. The men turned to look at the car entering their domain.

Krista watched the scene with dull eyes. Was being taken in by the rear door a good or bad sign?

"One moment, miss." Ted Black stepped out of the car. He wanted to check there were no horse droppings on the pathway leading to the rear entrance. He had sisters. He knew how they would react to stepping into a mess in their good shoes. He walked around the car, his eyes examining the cobbles. "If you would, miss." He opened the rear door and stood waiting for the young woman to step out of the car. He didn't know why he'd been ordered to bring her through this entrance and up the back stairway. It wasn't his place to question his superiors.

"I'll park the car and join you, Ted!" the driver called through the open window of the car. "I'm sure you can handle things from here!" The girl didn't look dangerous to him. She'd sat good as gold for the ten-minute car journey.

Ted escorted the girl up three flights of bare stairs with unadorned grey walls. "In here, miss." He opened an unmarked door. "Someone will be with you presently." He closed the door and took up position in the hallway to one side of the closed door. He tried not to sigh. That young woman wasn't likely to do a runner but he had his orders.

Krista crossed the bare floorboards, the sound of her heels echoing around the bare space. She walked towards the dusty window that was the only source of light in the room. She looked down on the stable yard without interest. She turned her back to the view to examine the room. A heavy wooden table – worn and

43

sad – sat almost exactly in the middle of the room, a single wooden chair tucked under the longest section, its back to the window. A bare bulb swung on thick electric cord from the ceiling.

She was being given time to contemplate her sins. She almost laughed. The woman she had thought was her mother, Madame Dumas, had used just such scare tactics to terrify her children into confessing their sins. Well, she had done nothing wrong. She had nothing to confess. She raised her chin unconsciously. She waited, wondering again why she was here. The silence in the room began to press in on her.

She started to pace but stopped herself. The sound of her pacing would be clearly heard by anyone who might like to listen. She didn't believe that she was free to walk out that unlocked door. She looked at the door, then very deliberately put her hand on the back of the single chair and began to drag the legs across the bare floor towards the window.

The door opened and the policeman who had escorted her here stood in the opening.

"Is everything all right in here?"

"I was going to sit down to look out the window," Krista said.

The sweet smile didn't fool Ted Black for a moment. The girl was not weeping and wailing. She was angry if he was any judge. He didn't know what she had done to attract the attention of the men in the SIS but they were making a mistake giving her time to think. But nobody asked him.

"If I had known I would be sitting and waiting I would have brought my knitting." She didn't knit. "Do they not say the devil tempts idle hands?" She had proved her point to herself. She was under guard. Why?

"Yes, miss." Ted Black stepped back out of the room, pulling the door closed.

Krista put her bag and gloves on the windowsill then sat down to wait. She would watch the police horses being groomed and try to stop her mind running in circles.

The door to the room slammed open and banged against the wall, almost knocking plaster off the wall. Krista didn't jump at this rude entrance. She had heard the men talking softly in the hall. The man who entered the room almost disappeared into his surroundings. He was short and slim with blonde hair and pale, pale skin. His grey suit was almost the shade of the walls of the room. He was completely forgettable until you saw his eyes. The fierce glare of a raptor over a hooked nose attracted the attention and held it. He was carrying a bulging brown-paper-covered folder that he slammed onto the table, sending a cloud of dust flying into the air.

"Chair!" He clicked his fingers behind him in the direction of Ted Black who had leaned in to close the door.

The man never took his eyes off Krista, examining her where she sat with her hands in her lap, legs bent decorously at the knee and off to the side. The serene image she presented in difficult circumstances pleased him. She might prove to be an asset to him after all. He'd doubted it when he'd learned of her past. She had grown up in a glorified inn, serving sweaty workmen coffee and cigarettes. That was not the kind of woman he needed.

"You are the woman calling herself Krista Grace Lestrange." He waited for her to speak while Black carried a chair into the room. He clicked his fingers again and pointed to where he wanted the chair, never removing his eyes from Krista. "Get that chair, Black." He pointed towards where Krista sat.

"Would you mind, miss?" Ted Black put his hand on the back of the chair Krista was sitting on.

"Certainly." Krista stood slowly, smiling over her shoulder at the policeman.

"Put it there," the grey man, as Krista was coming to think of him, snapped at the policeman. He focused on Krista again. "I was told you spoke English so why have you ignored my question?"

"I didn't hear a question." Krista refused to be intimidated. She intended to start as she meant to go on. "I heard a statement."

Ted Black placed the second chair across the table from the first and hurried out of the room. He wished he could be a fly on the wall for this interrogation. Antagonising the witness didn't seem to him to be the way to get the information you wanted but, then, what did he know?

"Sit down." A manicured finger pointed to the chair which was facing into the light coming from the unscreened window.

Krista collected her bag and gloves then walked across the floor. She put the bag and gloves on the table in front of her before taking the chair indicated. When she was once more seated, she pulled the brim of her hat lower, shading her eyes from the glare coming off the window glass.

"My name is Clarence Brown." The grey man told the lie without blinking. "I had you brought here. I will ask again, are you the female calling herself Krista Grace Lestrange?" He opened the folder on the desk.

"I am."

"Do you know why you are here?" He glared.

"I do not."

He almost smiled. She wasn't in the least frightened of him – and she should be. He allowed the silence to become uncomfortable while making a pretence of studying the papers in front of him.

"You entered this country illegally," he snapped, watching carefully to see if she flinched. She didn't.

"I did." There was no point in denying it. He obviously knew already. She didn't rush into explanation but waited to see what would happen next.

"You entered this country with a German aristocrat Herr Baron von Furstenberg." He waited a moment. The information his staff had gathered on this girl was almost unbelievable. "Your uncle, I believe."

"No." She almost laughed.

"You did not enter this country with the Baron?"

"I did, yes." Again, why deny what he already knew? "But the Baron is no relation of mine."

"His deceased brother was your father." The grey man felt almost sorry for her but in these times one must do what was needed. "That, I believe, makes the Baron your uncle."

"No. My parents died when I was a baby, sir," Krista said. "I know no more than that."

"Your father." He slapped a large studio photograph on the tabletop in front of her.

She leaned forward, examining the photograph, her heart thundering in her chest. Could something so outrageous be true?

"He," he tapped the photograph with one beautiful long-fingered hand, "was the elder brother of the man you know as Baron von Furstenberg. The title was his," again he tapped the picture, "until his death when the current Baron inherited the title."

"You believe this man has something to do with me?" She was trying to understand what she – a girl raised in an *auberge de ville* – could have to do with a titled family. It was ludicrous. She liked that word – ludicrous – Lia used it frequently.

"I not only believe," the man calling himself Clarence Brown said, "I *know* that man is your father. The affair between your mother and father was a well-known fact in some social circles." He could see she didn't believe him. Time to hit her with the rest of it. He slapped another studio photograph onto the table. "The late Baron's family. His wife and two daughters." A quick tap of the image. "You cannot tell from a black-and-white photograph but you share hair and eye-colouring with your half-sisters."

Krista couldn't speak. Her eyes were glued to the pretty image of an older woman with a smiling face sitting between two young women who shared a family resemblance. All three stared and smiled into the camera. Were these young women really relations of hers?

Before she could recover from the shock, another photograph was slammed onto the table.

"Your mother." He couldn't allow her time to gather her composure. "Lady Constance Stowe-Grenville, the only daughter of Viscount Cuthbert Stowe-Grenville and granddaughter of the Duke of Stowe-Grenville." He could almost pity the young woman as her shaking fingers reached out to touch the beautiful face in the black-and-white studio photograph. She didn't appear to hear the impressive titles. The Stowe-Grenville family were leading lights in British society.

"Why are you telling me this?" Krista couldn't take her eyes off the smiling face of the woman in the photograph. She looked like an imp of mischief in the image. Was she really her mother? How could this man know so much about her when she knew next to nothing?

"You are half German, half English yet you claim to be French," was all the answer she received.

"I was raised by a French family in France." She had to force her eyes to leave the image of the woman this man claimed was her mother. Was there a resemblance or was she deluding herself? She shrugged and raised injured blue eyes to the man tormenting her with his superior knowledge. She had learned already that the Dumas family were no relations of hers – for which she gave thanks. Miss Andrews had hinted she knew more about Krista's past but had never spoken in detail about what she knew. Was any of this ridiculous story possible?

"Your late father was German. You entered this country with a German aristocrat. I could have you arrested and held as an enemy alien."

"Is it possible to arrest someone for something they had no knowledge of?" Krista was past being frightened. The information this man shared with her had shocked her, yes, but, really, what did it change about her life? She was still alone in a strange country.

49

She had no one to depend on but herself. This information changed nothing about those facts. She was grateful for the help she had received from Miss Andrews and the people she'd met in this country but her fate was ultimately in her own hands. "You did not have me brought here to tell me about these people." She waved a hand at the photographs sitting on the table. She could not believe the strangers in the photographs were related to her. "Why am I here?" She met the raptor glare, refusing to drop her eyes.

"You appear to have amassed a number of very influential friends in the short time you have been in this country." Clarence Brown was impressed with her control of her reactions. How would he react if someone showed him photographs claiming they were close relations? He was surprised to realise that he would have to give careful thought to the matter. He simply did not know.

"I don't understand what you mean, I'm afraid."

"An application for British citizenship has been made in your name."

"Has it?" Krista fought the urge to shrug. "My guardian Miss Violet Andrews made mention of her intention to apply for papers in my name. I have no further knowledge of the matter." She hadn't heard anything further about the application.

"You were unaware that Winston Churchill signed the official request?" Clarence Brown wondered how this young woman had so many people of stature willing to put their names and reputations forward. It was so unusual that it had caught his attention. He did not care for situations he did not understand.

Krista disguised her surprise. "I have told you all I know." She sat back in the chair and waited. "If there are problems with the paperwork you may consult Miss Andrews. I can supply you with her telephone number."

"There is no need. I have it." Clarence Brown waited for the girl sitting so calmly across the table from him to demand particulars of the nobility he had told her were her relations. Surely, she would want to contact some of them – ask for assistance? As far as he could discover, she was penniless and working for a very small wage. When she remained silent he was impressed. Yes, indeed, he could use her.

"I will have the police escort you home." He busied himself pushing copies of the studio photographs of her parents into a large brown envelope he took from the file in front of him. He slipped in a photograph of the two at an Embassy ball together. A child should know her parents in his opinion. "You may take this." He held the envelope across the table.

"Thank you." Krista stood to take the envelope. "If I am free to leave I have no need of an escort. I would prefer to walk back to my employer's house. It is not far." She tried not to run from the room.

"I will be in touch."

The soft words followed her out of the room. Promise or threat. She didn't know and right now she couldn't care. She just wanted to leave this place.

Chapter 6

While Krista was being interrogated in a dusty room at the back of New Scotland Yard, Perry was sitting in a great deal more comfort in his father's Whitehall gentlemen's club.

"It is early for an alcoholic beverage according to society's rules but I'll be dashed if I'll sit here over a pot of tea!" Admiral Sir Henry Fotheringham-Carter leaned back in his deep leather chair. He stared across a gleaming round table at his youngest son. The only one of his children to resemble him so forcefully. It was uncanny to his eyes to see himself recreated in another.

"It is not often I am summoned to accompany you to your club, Pater." Perry watched a servant carrying a silver tray walk across the richly coloured thick-pile carpet in the direction of their table.

"I have ordered drinks and cigars for us both."

The two men remained silent while the drinks, cigars and a thick glass ashtray were put on the table. When they had been served each man cut the top off a cigar. When both cigars were lit they puffed grey smoke towards the ceiling.

"I have been assured – repeatedly – by your tutors that you have a brain." Sir Henry narrowed his light-brown eyes in his son's direction. "I have never seen any indication of this myself." This son of his had been the despair of his tutors and professors. They had insisted he had a first-class brain but refused to apply himself. He had smiled charmingly and done exactly as he pleased.

"Because I enjoy sailing but refuse to make the sea my career." This was not a new discussion between them.

"The Horse Guards!" Sir Henry snorted. "I have never understood your fascination with sitting on the back of a horse looking pretty."

Perry held his cigar between his teeth and grinned at his father's disgust. The old man believed there was only one serving force – the Navy – anything else was unacceptable. "Now, sir, that is prejudice pure and simple."

"I don't want to see a son of mine prancing about on a horse dressed like a toy soldier!" Sir Henry snapped.

"That will not happen now, Pater." Perry gestured at his leg stretched to one side of him. He had been schooling an untried horse over jumps. The animal refused the jump and somehow managed to trap its front legs in the crossbars of the fence. Fence and horse had collapsed, trapping Perry's leg underneath. It was only the prompt action of a groom that prevented further injury.

"I told you repeatedly that prancing around on horses would never lead to anything good." Sir Henry narrowed his eyes against the smoke from his cigar. It hurt his heart to see his son limping around the place.

"It was an accident pure and simple, Pater." Perry was tired of this old argument. It would change nothing. His leg was permanently damaged and he had to find some way to live with that fact. He did not need constant reminders of his misfortune.

"We have seen little of you this summer." Sir Henry needed to move the conversation along. He had not summoned his son here to berate him. He had become rather involved in talks himself this past summer. If his son had visited the family estate he would not have been home.

"I spent a great deal of the summer performing escort duties and being messenger boy for some very determined ladies."

"I beg your pardon?" Sir Henry leaned forward and pointed with his cigar. "No son of mine runs messages – explain yourself, sir."

"I became somewhat involved with a group of ladies determined to remove children from danger in Europe. Having time on my hands, I was free to escort ladies around London and carry messages when necessary." He had enjoyed knowing he was helping in his own small way.

"That damned Hitler!" Sir Henry sipped his whiskey and remained silent for a moment, studying his son. It was time to fish or cut bait, he thought. "He is going to take us into war, you know."

"I know." Perry looked at his leg, stifling his frustration. What use would he be in a fighting force? He wanted to curse fate.

"You studied German and French at school, did you not?" Sir Henry was aware of his son's interests. It had been difficult to keep the boy sitting at a desk. He always wanted to be outside. That had not prevented him from receiving a first-class education.

"I barely scrapped past." Perry regretted his lack of attention to his courses now. He had been frustrated listening to Krista switch languages with such ease.

"None the less you have some knowledge of the subjects."

"Father, what is this all about?" Perry knew his father. He was steering the conversation in this direction for a reason.

"There will be need of men with a knowledge of languages." Sir Henry had been surprised to be approached about his son by someone high in government circles. "There is more to fighting than pointing a gun." Sir Henry had been given notice that he would be called back into service if war should be declared.

"Pater, would you please just come to the point of this meeting?" Perry almost slapped his hand on the tabletop.

"The government is setting up intensive language courses for certain people," Sir Henry said. "Just how bad was your French and German?"

"I was quite all right with the written word and could read reasonably well but I failed miserably when

I tried to get my tongue around the languages." He looked at his father shamefaced. "I didn't try particularly hard."

"As I thought." He pointed to the injured leg. "That, my boy, has changed your fate. There is no getting away from the fact."

"I do know that, sir."

"If I can see that you are offered a place on these specialised courses in languages," he leaned across to pin his son in place with a glare that had frightened seamen for years, "will you apply yourself?"

"To what purpose, sir?" Perry needed a reason to study. He had excelled in anything that could challenge his way of thinking and improve his knowledge of his own affairs but poetry and languages had seemed like a terrible waste of time he could be using for another purpose entirely. He had done the minimum required to pass and been thankful to leave all of that behind him.

"You have always been the most physically active one of my children." Sir Henry looked at the well-set-up young man who had run wild for most of his life. "That," again he pointed to the injured leg, "has put a halt to your gallop. You need to find a new direction – a new purpose for your life."

"I agree." A picture of Krista flashed across his mind. Her beautiful face so serious at their first meeting when she informed him she was deciding her fate. "I will willingly accept any advice and counsel offered."

"I have been informed by many throughout your young life that you are an exceedingly handsome and charming young man. A credit to the family name."

"That is self-flattery, sir," Perry laughed. This was

the strangest conversation he had ever had with his father. "Mama assures me that I am a carbon copy of your good self."

"Be that as it may," Sir Henry waved that aside, "you may well look like me, young man, but to a group of people who have made a study of you it would appear you have also inherited your mother's excellent brain."

"Mama?" Perry loved his mother. The woman was everything feminine and charming. She ran the family estate with stunning skill. The thought of his mother being considered of above average intelligence quite overshadowed the mention of anyone making a study of him. He was nothing remarkable.

"Your mother was in naval intelligence in the last war." Sir Henry smiled to remember the young Wren who had run rings around some of the brightest of the back-room boys.

"Mama?"

"Yes, boy, your mother." Sir Henry gestured to Peregrine to lean closer, looking around to check that they could not be overheard. This was a gentlemen's club but one could never be too careful – not in today's climate. "You have come to the notice of a particular branch of the government."

"I have?" What on earth had he done to attract anyone's attention? Surely there were more important matters going on in the world than anything he might get up to?

"Do you see why I doubt your intelligence?" Sir Henry had to force himself to keep his voice down. This youngest son of his frustrated him. "Have I not already mentioned that people have made a study of you?"

"Yes, sir."

"You have been seen in the company of a German woman." Sir Henry glared. "Have you no sense? Our country will soon be at war with Germany."

"The young woman I imagine you mean, Pater, is French." Perry narrowed his eyes and had he but known it gave his father a glare identical to his own from eyes that glowed almost amber. "I may well have been in company with women who are of German descent this summer. They are women willing to risk much to help children escape from Hitler's clutches." He hadn't made special note of the nationality of the women involved in helping the children. Who on earth had been watching him? He hadn't noticed anyone in particular but, then, he hadn't been looking.

"Yes, yes, that is all very well." Sir Henry took a slip of paper from his inside breast pocket. He had no wish to know of his son's paramours. "You are to present yourself to this address." He pushed the paper across the table. He held on to it when Peregrine reached out to take it. "It is imperative that you study hard. You must speak and understand German and French when you complete this course. I have been asked to tell you no more but I was allowed to make mention of the course in the hopes that I could stir you to apply yourself. The fate of many people will depend upon your success."

Perry began to remove the paper from under his father's fingers, never removing his eyes from his father's face. The man was not one to make dramatic statements. Was he being offered some way to serve his country? How would a knowledge of foreign languages help? He thought of his former professors of language and stifled a groan.

"Before you present yourself at this address," Sir Henry tapped the paper he still held, "Gilligan wants to see you."

Perry stared. Gilligan was their saddle-maker. "Why?"

"I have no idea. I was merely asked to pass along the message." Sir Henry shrugged. "He asks that you present yourself as soon as possible. I suggest you take a quick moment to see what the man wants. Heaven knows he has made enough saddles for you through the years."

"Yes, sir." Perry sat back and puffed his cigar. What an odd morning. What did it all mean? He mentally shrugged. He would find out no doubt.

"You should also make time to visit your mother." Sir Henry felt he had accomplished what was needed. It was up to his son now.

Krista was so relieved to exit the bewildering maze of hallways that were hidden behind the red-brick façade of New Scotland Yard and out into the light of day that she almost cried aloud.

She thought briefly of telephoning the Caulfield home to inform them she was on her way back but had decided against the idea. She needed time alone, time to think. She had to process the information she had been given. Could it be true?

Everything in her life had been changed from the moment she had heard the man she thought of as her father agree to allow her – no, she had to be brutally truthful even in her own thoughts – Monsieur Dumas had seemed almost gleeful as he offered her up to a man known for his aggressive and unhealthy appetites towards the defenceless.

She had been trying so hard not to dwell on her time with the Dumas family. When she had discovered she was not related to them she had been relieved. Now, to discover she was related to members of the nobility – what did that mean? Did it mean anything? They had not wanted her. She had been fobbed off on the Dumas family. Should she not be grateful for the roof over her head and the food in her mouth? There were many much worse off than she.

She walked through the park, blind to the beauty around her. She didn't hear the birds sing. She failed to see the people who walked past her with a nod of greeting. She was deaf and blind to everything in her path, her mind trying desperately to process what the grey man had told her.

Why had she been called into that office? It had all been so strange – very cloak and dagger.

Miss Andrews had told her she knew her mother and father. It was she who had told her that her parents were deceased. Did she know more? Why hadn't she told all she knew? It would have been kinder not to allow her discover the truth about herself from a stranger.

If the grey man's name was Brown she was a monkey's uncle. The man had lied about his name, she was sure, without blinking. If he could lie so fluently what else had he lied about? What did he want with her?

Krista continued to stroll unseeing through the park, her mind seemingly chasing itself in circles as she tried to make sense of the new information. What did it change, if anything? What did that man want of her? She was convinced he wanted something. He had not bothered to arrange to meet her simply to tell her what he knew.

"Krista!" Miss Andrews' her voice rang out with relief from the open door of the drawing room as soon as Krista stepped through the door of the Caulfield home.

"Let the poor girl come inside." Lia came from behind Miss Andrews and, with a soft smile in Krista's direction, took the other woman's arm. "Run upstairs and remove your outer clothing, Krista. I will have Cook serve a pot of tea. Come down and join us as soon as you are ready." The unspoken words '*and you can tell us all*' were clearly inferred.

Chapter 7

Krista resisted the urge to slam the door to her room.
She wished she had the luxury to dramatically tear the
outfit she was wearing from her body and throw it on
the floor. Her flesh was crawling. She wanted to scrub
the memory of this morning from her skin.

She put her hat, gloves and handbag on top of the
tallboy. She didn't want to open the large brown envelope
the grey man had given her. Not yet. She needed time to
assimilate the information about her past first.

She kicked off her shoes and sat on the bed to
carefully remove her silk stockings, trying desperately
not to even think.

She removed her clothes with care, folding them and
putting them on a chair. She would hang the dress and

coat in the bathroom when she had her bath. The steam from the bathwater should freshen them up. The undergarments and silk stockings she would handwash. She could not afford to ruin clothing in a temper tantrum – much as she might want to. "*Enough,*" she hissed to herself in French.

She pushed her legs into the navy pleated slacks she'd been wearing when the police came to the house. Then put on the knitted twinset in pale blue with navy accents, socks and saddle-stitched navy walking shoes and was once more as she had been before the shocks of the morning.

"They are all sitting downstairs waiting for me," she said to herself, dragging a brush carelessly through her hair. "They will be expecting me to tell them everything." She threw the hairbrush onto the bed with such force it bounced. "They tell me nothing but I must share my every thought!" She stared at the clock she'd bought from a pawnshop. "How can it not yet be time to pick up the boys from school? This morning has been as long as a year. Yet the boys will only be finishing their lunch. How is that possible?"

The rest of the household had been watching and wondering about Krista all morning. It wasn't every day the police called to a respectable house.

"Did you get a chance to have a word with Krista since she came back?" Wilma checked a casserole she had bubbling away in the oven.

"No, I didn't even get a look at her," Peggy was sitting at the kitchen table. "I was in the dining room getting it set up for lunch. The mistress said that lot," she jerked her chin in the direction of the front of the house, "would most likely be staying for lunch. I don't suppose Krista has had bit, bite nor sup since she left here."

"I've boiled the kettle that many times this morning the arse will be boiled out of it." Wilma checked on the serving dishes in the warming oven. "I can't imagine what the police would want with our Krista. There isn't an ounce of malice in that girl."

"We can wonder and worry all we like but until she tells us what's going on we are in the dark." Peggy's nerves were in ribbons, she was that worried for a girl she'd come to like and think of as a friend.

"Peggy, Wilma, she has come down." Lia was standing at the door of the kitchen.

Wilma and Peggy were startled. Normally the mistress would have rung for them if she wanted anything.

"How does she seem in herself?" Wilma asked.

"Is she alright?" Peggy's words came over Wilma's.

"I don't know." Lia looked back over her shoulder. "The others are waiting to speak with her. I know no more now than we did this morning. I'm sure she'll come down to the kitchen for a cup of tea after that pair," she jerked her head towards the dining room, "have finished with her." She shared a glance with her staff and with a sigh turned to go. "Well, we are ready to eat. Do you need me to carry anything up to the dining room?"

"I already have everything we might need on the sideboards in the dining room." Peggy stood up and shook out her fancy white apron. "It won't take me a minute to get everything ready."

"We can serve ourselves, Peggy." Lia walked out of the kitchen with Peggy at her heels. "I didn't invite these women to dine after all. We are all perfectly capable of filling a plate for ourselves. I don't have an army of servants as my brother does."

Abigail looked from her own well-filled plate of casserole and fresh vegetables to the tiny portion of food Krista has served herself. "Krista – *that*," she pointed at the plate with her fork, "is not enough to keep a bird alive."

"I am not very hungry." Krista had a lump in her throat. She sipped from the glass of water in front of her, wishing for a glass of full-bodied red wine.

"Was this morning dreadful for you?" Violet had rushed to the Caulfield home, wanting to be with Krista when she returned. She had no idea how to help the pale-faced young girl sitting like a mannequin across the table from her.

"I am struggling to understand what this morning was all about." Krista watched the women at the table with her eat elegantly while never seeming to remove their eyes from her face. "I have never been hit around the head repeatedly, but I imagine how I am feeling right now must be a similar sensation to that act of violence."

"What did the police want of you?" Lia was concerned for Krista of course but she needed to know if this morning's activities could affect her husband's career. She had never been visited by the police before.

"The man I met with was not a police officer," Krista said softly. "He introduced himself to me as Clarence Brown, a government official. He did not do me the courtesy of telling me which arm of the government he represented. He looked at me like something that had crawled from under a rock." She looked across the table at Violet and Abigail. "He made mention of an application for papers in my name. He appeared to think I was some class of enemy alien trying to obtain papers fraudulently." She almost sobbed but refused to allow herself to break down in this company.

"Did he indeed?" Abigail's knuckles turned white on her silver cutlery.

"He showed me photographs of people he claimed were my parents." Krista pushed her plate away. She couldn't eat. She simply could not. She watched the colour leach out of the women's faces. They all knew. Everyone seated at this table seemed to know all about her. How was that possible when she knew nothing – nothing! "They were both apparently members of the nobility."

"Oh, my dear!" Violet rested her cutlery on her plate. "I am so sorry. It is my fault. I have been a coward."

"You told me you knew both my parents." Krista couldn't even find it in herself to be angry. "You said they were both deceased. Is that true?"

"Yes, my dear." Violet's eyes were moist. "Everything I told you was the truth. I withheld certain information because I simply did not know how to tell you all I knew. I am so sorry you found out this way. What that man did to you is unforgivable."

"I think, Lia," Krista said slowly, "that I should look for another position. I do not wish to bring trouble to your door."

"*No!*" Abigail snapped.

"*My dear!*" Violet was horrified.

"Krista, we need to take some time to think about this. The boys and everyone in the house would miss you terribly."

"I walked home through the park and thought about the meeting I had with that man." She gave the company a half smile. "I think of him as the grey man. Everything about him was grey except for his eyes. They were the eyes of a raptor. They made me shiver. I have seen films at the picture house of raptors as they tear apart their prey. I was that man's prey. Of that I have no doubt."

There was silence at the table as all digested her words. Abigail now knew who Krista had met with. She knew the grey man with the eyes of a bird of prey. Indeed she did. What on earth could he want with Krista?

"Lia," Abigail pushed her plate from her – she had made quite a dent in the food. "I asked you to take Krista –"

"Asked?" Lia gave a choked laugh.

"Yes." Abigail glared. "*Asked* you to take someone with no official papers into your home. I know you are worried that this morning's happenings could have a negative effect on Charles career – how could you not?"

"The thought has crossed my mind." Lia wouldn't deny it. Her husband was a career navy man. He had risen in the ranks and aspired to rise higher.

"I don't know – yet – what game is being played here." Abigail glanced at Violet. "I will find out. That I can assure you." She held up a dimpled hand when it appeared Lia would interrupt. "Having Krista in your home will not adversely affect Charles or your good self. I would not have dreamed of asking you to shelter her if that had been the case."

Krista sat quietly listening, wondering if her head could actually explode.

"Krista," Violet leaned forward to capture Krista's eyes. She wanted her to see her sincerity. "Your mother was a dear, dear friend to both Abigail and me." She saw Abigail nod out of the corner of her eye. "We feel, both of us, that we failed your mother and you. That is not an excuse. It is simple fact." She had tried to think of a way to break the news of her parentage to Krista without harming the girl who was innocent in all of this. She had left it too late and look what had happened.

"The news of your mother's death," Abigail had to stop for a moment to gather her composure, "devastated both Violet and me. It caused shockwaves to ripple through everyone who knew her. She was dearly loved by a great many people."

Krista didn't know what to say, how to react. She had never known the woman they spoke of.

"We grieved," Violet put her hand over Abigail's on the table, "both of us in our own way. But in our grief we failed your mother." She bit back a sob. The memories of that time were still painful.

"Is that when you ..." Lia was thinking frantically back to that time. "You took to your bed, Abigail. I remember. It frightened me to see you laid so low."

Krista could practically feel the sorrow in the room. Yet she, who surely had been the most affected, could only watch and wonder. She felt trapped in a fairy tale. The strict, almost abusive people who raised her were no relations of hers. Her parents were titled gentry. She stifled a laugh. Miss Andrews had introduced her class of children learning English to the writer Edgar Rice

Burroughs. He wrote about Tarzan of the Apes. A child who had been lost in the jungle after the death of its parents. What did that make her – Krista of the Auberge?

She stood and began to clear the table. The others stared at her, surprised by her sudden move.

"I am not running away from this conversation," she assured them. "I simply thought it time to clear the dishes. Peggy and Cook will be waiting to eat their own meal." She picked up the crockery before anyone could stop her and left the dining room.

She used her hip to push open the kitchen door. She carried the dishes past the staring servants and put them on the draining board.

"Krista ..." Peggy didn't know what to say.

"Peggy is the one who should be clearing the table," Wilma said.

"Let me do that, Cook." Krista turned to look at the two women who had befriended her. "Things are all mixed up at the moment. I'll take a tray and clear away if you don't mind." She didn't wait for permission but grabbed a tray and left the kitchen.

Upstairs, she cleared the remains of the meal onto the large tray. "Ladies," she asked, "do you want tea or coffee?"

"Coffee, I think – Lia, don't you?" Abigail was watching Krista closely. Was she really so unaffected by this morning's revelations? "With a dash of cognac for the nerves."

The dining room had been cleared. The four women were sitting in the family room. Krista had run upstairs to fetch the photographs the grey man had given her. She had discovered the additional photograph and stared at it for a moment. She'd returned it to the envelope, deciding she would study it on her own later. She'd carried two of the photographs downstairs and put both photographs on the coffee table separating the four comfortable chairs grouped around it.

"Are these people truly my parents?" She took a seat beside Lia, staring across the coffee table at Violet and Abigail.

Violet leaned forward and touched the edge of the photograph of the woman and her daughters with only the tip of one finger.

"The grey man threw them onto the table between us," Krista went on. "He stated that the woman portrayed in the photograph was my mother." She was shaking internally, her every nerve-ending quivering. "He then went on to give me details he insisted I already knew."

"I don't understand." Abigail looked not at the photographs but Krista. "I believe I know the identity of what you call the grey man. He is intense but I have never known him to be intentionally cruel and what he subjected you to this morning was cruel."

"I have had time now to think about his actions," Krista said. "I believe – for whatever reason – he was testing me."

"It is all very confusing." Abigail did not like to be confused. She would make enquiries.

"Do you not see how strongly you resemble your mother, Krista?" Violet had not been paying attention to the conversation. She was riveted by the image that portrayed her friend so well.

"I have not had time to study the image." Krista glanced at the clock. "I do not have time now. I must pick the children up from school." She almost ran from the room.

Chapter 8

"Have you heard any more about your papers, Krista?"
Peggy was muffled against the cold dark October
evening.

"I am still waiting to hear." It had been ten days since
Krista had been taken to Old Scotland Yard. She had
told Peggy and Mrs Acers that it concerned a simple mix-
up over her papers – what else could she say?

The two young women were making their way back
to the Caulfield home from the centre set up to handle
affairs for the young refugees. Krista had spent the
evening translating letters from families desperate to
flee Europe. Peggy had been one of the many sorting
through donated clothing and toys. Lia was taking care
of the boys.

"My heart bleeds for the children being sent away from their homes – from everything they have ever known." Peggy didn't mind working a few nights a week to help out. "I didn't know if I was coming or going when I first went into service. It was the first time I'd ever been away from home. Can you imagine what these poor children must be feeling? It doesn't bear thinking about."

"It will be easier for their parents and grandparents to make plans to leave without the children underfoot." Krista tucked her chin into the scarf Peggy had knit for her.

"Here," Peggy stopped a moment, the smoke-filled air closing in around her, "how come we haven't seen anything of your Perry?"

"He is on a course." Krista pulled at Peggy's arm to get her moving again. "Now you know all I know."

The two young women walked quickly along, exchanging remarks from time to time but each eager to get out of the dark night.

"I'll make a pot of hot chocolate when we get in." Peggy was searching through her coat pockets for the house key as they neared their destination. "Nothing better for helping you sleep." The evenings she worked at the centre gave her sleepless nights. She hated to think of all those young children being removed from their parents and put onto trains. They travelled for days across land and sea to a country they didn't know to live with strangers who spoke a language they didn't understand. Was it worth it?

They stripped off their outer wear in the kitchen. The range kept the big room warm. Peggy put a pot of milk on top of the range to heat. She'd shave pieces from the large slab of chocolate kept in the larder into the milk as it heated. Krista took heavy glass mugs out of the cupboard.

"Good evening, ladies!" Lia stepped into the kitchen. "Will there be enough chocolate for one more, Peggy?" She pulled a wooden chair away from the kitchen table.

"Won't take me a minute to add more milk, missus." Peggy was getting accustomed to her mistress joining them in the evening. Queer sort of carry-on, according to her mam but what was the poor woman supposed to do? Sit in lonely splendour all night?

Krista took another mug out of the cupboard and set it on the table.

"How were things at the centre this evening?" Lia sat and watched the two young women work together.

"We are getting a great number of letters from people who are not of the Jewish faith." Krista pulled out a chair and sat down.

Peggy carefully poured the hot chocolate into the mugs and shaved chocolate into curls over each. "It seems to me, listening to you two, that it isn't healthy living in Germany for anyone who disagrees with that Hitler." She carried the block of chocolate back towards the larder. It needed to stay cold.

"Bring the box of biscuits out with you, please, Peggy!" Lia called after her.

Krista pushed back her chair. She took side plates from the cupboard, put them on the table and sat back down.

Peggy carried the box of biscuits out of the larder and put it unopened onto the table.

"How are your hands, Krista?" Lia opened the biscuits and took a shortbread out before offering the tin to the others.

"They are still cramping after a long session of translating." Krista put her hands on the tabletop. "Mrs Acers has made a pomade for me to put on every night. It is helping." She slept in old cotton gloves she wore over the smelly substance. "I want to help in any way I can – the letters we are receiving are heart-breaking." She wrote out each translation in longhand which took time. She was slightly ambidextrous and changed hands frequently during her stint of translating. She wanted to translate as many letters as possible. She wasn't the only one suffering from clutching a pencil for hours.

"We are looking for ladies who know typewriting." Lia understood how difficult it was to step away from the thousands of pleading letters they were receiving. "It would be so much better to type up the translations rather than having you and the other translators write out each one."

They all three concentrated on their chocolate and biscuits. There was not a great deal they could do or say. All involved in removing children from danger were doing all that they could.

Lia's thoughts were running on a different track, however. She had a reason for coming down to the kitchen. There was something she needed to announce.

"I received a telephone call this evening, Krista," she said, taking another biscuit and trying to sound calm. "You and I are to present ourselves at government buildings in Whitehall tomorrow morning."

Krista dropped the biscuit she held, looking horrified.

"Maybe you'll be getting your papers at last?" Peggy suggested.

"We shan't know why they want us until we hear what they have to say." Lia had been given enough information to worry her. "We shall take the bus after we have dropped the boys off at school. It is not such a great distance."

"What should I wear?" Krista asked. After years of wearing what she thought of as her uniform in the café, having a choice of outfit could be confusing.

"We can decide that in the morning when we see what the weather is like."

"Ladies, thank you for coming." Graham Waters looked at the two women seated in front of his temporary desk. He threw the thick file he carried onto the desktop, fighting to keep the curse words he longed to utter locked behind his teeth. "I am Captain Graham Waters, and you are?"

As if he couldn't tell just by looking at them which was which. He didn't know a great deal about women's clothing but the difference in their social status was clear to his eyes. He almost rolled his eyes in exasperation. It would appear the backroom boys had been right. They had insisted they would need a woman's touch while deciding on clothing for this charade. He didn't understand fully why the social divide between the two women was so obvious to him. Was it only because of how they dressed and held themselves? He had never given the matter much thought. He only knew he'd instinctively noticed the difference.

"I am Cordelia Caulfield." Lia looked at the weary face of the man in uniform. What in heaven's name were they doing at the War Office? She waved a hand towards Krista sitting to her side. "My assistant Krista Lestrange."

"Indeed." Graham examined the young woman he'd been assured could carry out the mission he had planned. He should just get on with it. Time was of the essence. "According to my sources you ladies have been active in the associations concerned with the removal of children from German and occupied Austria. Is this correct?"

His words caused Krista and Lia to sit up straighter in their chairs. What had that to do with anything? They looked at each other before giving a nod of agreement towards the captain.

"As such you are both more aware of the state of affairs in Europe than most civilians." Graham took a deep breath. It was happening, months of planning and now he had to hand it to amateurs. "Ladies, you have been called here today because this country needs your help." He waited but, apart from staring at him, neither reacted.

"Miss Lestrange –" Graham switched to German, a language he spoke fluently. He had spent many enjoyable summers in Bavaria with his extended family. "Would you tell me a little about your life here in Great Britain?" He had been assured the woman spoke German but he preferred to discover her proficiency for himself. Too much depended on this.

He listened as Krista told him of her day-to-day life. He was not greatly interested but she did indeed speak German like a native. She looked German with that white hair that usually darkened when one left childhood. He held up his hand to stop her in mid-sentence. He had heard enough. He opened the file on his desk.

"Your mother was English." He spoke French now. "You arrived in this country without papers." He waited for her response. He listened as she answered him in fluid French. She did indeed speak both languages with ease.

"What is this all about, Captain?" Lia had watched his face while he questioned Krista.

"You need papers to stay in this country legally, do you not?" Graham spoke in English now, ignoring the question. "Those papers are being processed." He would not blackmail this young woman. He preferred to pay her for her help. "In the meantime, England needs your help. You can drive, I am told?"

"After a fashion," Krista answered in English. She had been taught to drive by Philippe Dumas after she'd begged and bribed him. They had taken the cars of the *auberge* guests for a spin when they could get away with it. She had never been on the road by herself. She wasn't confident of her skill. Did it matter?

Graham pinched the bridge of his nose. This was the best chance they would have. He looked at the two women. They had both been thoroughly investigated. He had to take a chance on both of them.

"Mrs Caulfield, you are here because we wish to remove Krista from your employ for a time." He held up a hand when the woman opened her mouth to question him further. He had no time. "I have been assured this will not cause you a great deal of difficulty. You will need to tell your household a story to cover Miss Lestrange's absence from your home."

"What exactly do you want of me, Captain?" Krista

77

couldn't imagine what she could do for Great Britain. She was French!

Graham stood. He couldn't sit behind a desk any longer. He needed to be doing something active. "Ladies, I need your assurance that what is discussed in this room will never be repeated."

"My husband –" Lia was cut off by another annoying wave of the captain's hand.

"Captain Caulfield has no need to know anything of this." Graham put his hands behind his back. "Miss Lestrange will be back in your home before the captain returns. This information must not be shared in a letter. Is that understood?"

"Perhaps you should tell us in greater detail what you expect of us?" Lia could see his doubts. They were written large across his face.

"If you both agree to help this country, Miss Lestrange will need weeks of intensive training. During that time, we ask that you, Mrs Caulfield, purchase an extensive wardrobe for her." He waved a hand between the two women. "We need Miss Lestrange to look as effortlessly glamorous as you yourself, Mrs Caulfield."

"Explain." Lia thought Krista looked very nice in her navy skirt suit and white blouse.

"I want you, Mrs Caulfield to dress your assistant like one of the many," again he pinched his nose, hoping to push back the headache, "debutantes you grew up with. She must be made to look and act like a social butterfly. A young woman from one of the best families who thinks only of clothing and gossip." He knew such women. His family pushed them in his direction at every opportunity. "It must be from the skin out." He almost blushed at her glare.

"There is a problem with that, Captain." Lia was becoming angry. Why could the man not simply state what was needed and leave them to figure out how or if they could achieve what he wanted? "Krista is not a polished airhead." She had fought all of her life it seemed from being forced into that mould herself.

"Mrs Caulfield, your country – *I* need your help," Graham practically snarled.

"Perhaps you should explain exactly what you want of me?" Lia said.

"I cannot – at this moment in time." Graham saw clearly what his fellow strategists saw in this woman. She was far from a lightweight butterfly. "I can only tell you both that I need Miss Lestrange to agree to enter into training for a mission that will be explained in full – if and it is a big if – she passes the training."

Krista watched the pair lock horns and wondered when they would remember that she was in the room. It was her life that they were bandying around.

"So, let me see if I understand," Lia took a deep breath, "from the little you've told me. I am to answer any questions put to me about Krista's absence from my home while at the same time purchasing a full wardrobe of designer clothing for her to wear. Have I got that right?"

"Yes."

"Without explanation."

"Yes."

"This is all passing strange." Lia wanted to know more but if this was truly to serve her country – could she say no?

"Excuse me." Krista felt like putting up her hand as

they had in school when trying to attract the teacher's attention. "Haven't both of you forgotten something?"

"*What?*" they said in unison.

"*Me*," Krista gulped.

Chapter 9

"Are you certain you wish to do this, Krista?"

Lia sat on the bed watching Krista carefully fold the clothing she would not be taking with her into her large leather suitcase. The boys were in bed. Peggy was visiting her family. Mrs Acers had returned to her own home.

"Let us be honest," Krista paused in her packing, "I was foisted onto you." She shook her head when Lia started to object. "No, no. Honestly – I am not of a great deal of help to you. You have given me so much. You welcomed me into your home. You took me with you to your exercise classes. You introduced me to your friends. You have helped me adjust to my new life. I can never repay you for all you have done for me, Lia."

"You are mistaken," Lia said. "The benefits go both

ways. Your company these last months has been a true blessing. I had not realised how lonely I had become. It is difficult being the wife of a seafaring man. I knew that when I married, of course. I became caught up in the life of my boys – but since they started their schooling ..." She looked at the young girl who had become a friend. "Your company has helped me enormously. I ask again, Krista – are you quite certain you want to do this? They are offering you a paltry amount of money for something that may endanger your very life."

Krista resumed her packing, trying to think of how she could answer. The money offered to her for taking part in this adventure might seem paltry to Lia but a hundred pounds was a fortune to her. She would lodge the money in her post office account until her return. The money would give her a freedom of choice she had never had before. An added bonus – she could keep the designer wardrobe. But it wasn't only the money and clothes that attracted her. She would enjoy the adventure. How many days had she spent in the *auberge de ville* praying for something exciting to happen? Her escape from the *auberge* had been a matter of desperation not choice. This was her chance for a true adventure and she was taking it.

"Should I take these?" She held up the knee-length shorts she had used for attending the exercise classes with Lia.

"I would not." Lia laughed. "You have quite marvellous legs but do you really want to be wearing those," she pointed to the shorts. "around hairy-handed men." She fell onto the bed in a fit of giggles.

The more Krista stared, the more Lia laughed until tears came to her eyes.

"What on earth is the matter with you?"

"I had a vision of you wearing the navy knickers we wore for exercise at school." Lia put her fist to her mouth but the laughter still pouring out. "The knickers were thick and came to the knee. They were tied off with elastic. We called them passion-killers."

"You can be very silly." Krista smiled and returned to her packing. She had been told to bring only the basics and any slacks she might own. The clothes she was so proud of were deemed unsuitable for the role she was to play right now. The clothes would be stored in the attic here until she returned.

The household had been told she was off to visit some newly discovered English relatives.

"Now what am I supposed to do with a daffodil like you?" The army sergeant glared at Krista standing stiffly before him. "I am Sergeant Quinn – you will address me at all times as 'Sergeant' – is that clear?"

"Certainly, Sergeant."

Krista had been brought by car to a manor house deep in the English countryside. A scattering of army huts decorated the landscape. The fields were muddy and damp, the dark October day not inviting anyone to linger. She had been given a cup of tea and something to eat in the main house, surrounded by people who expressed no interest in her or what she was doing there.

"Look at you!" The sergeant pointed. "I was ordered to check your level of fitness. You look like you are getting ready for a stroll around Mayfair." He was shorter than Krista and had to stand on his toes to glare into her eyes. His handlebar moustache bristled with his outrage. "You will be crying for your mammy if I ask you to crawl through mud in that lot." Again he pointed at what Krista wore. "Come with me!" He turned to march away, not checking to see if she followed.

In her duffle coat over her navy-blue pleated slacks and blue knitted twinset, Krista shivered through the walk towards one of the outbuildings.

"*Doyle!*" The sergeant shouted as he pushed the door to the supply building open. "*Doyle, front and centre!*"

"You bellowed, Sarge!" An older man shuffled out of the stacks. He caught sight of Krista and smiled. "Aren't you a sight for sore eyes!"

"None of that nonsense!" the sergeant barked. "I want this one kitted out with battledress." He slapped the counter that stretched across the open space. "*Now!*"

"Battledress, Sarge – for a woman!"

"Battledress. She can't run around the fields in that …" Words seemed to fail him as he once more pointed at Krista.

"If you would remove your coat and step forward, please, miss?" Doyle leaned over the counter to examine Krista. "You're long in the leg."

"We'll have none of that," barked the sergeant.

"I have to look, Sarge, to see what size is needed." Doyle turned towards the stacks of folded uniforms and began removing items that he placed onto the countertop. "How many sets of each, Sarge?"

"Three, one on, one in the laundry and one clean." Quinn hadn't been told how long he would have this girl under his command but he knew she would need the proper clothes if there was any hope of him checking out her level of fitness. He didn't know what the world was coming to when he was asked to train a female.

Krista stood and watched the pile of neatly folded items grow. How was she supposed to carry all of that? As if in answer to her mental question, a kitbag joined the growing pile.

"What size boots, Sarge?" Doyle looked at the saddle-stitched navy-leather shoes that Krista wore. "I don't know if I have any small enough."

"Give her your smallest size. She can wear a couple of pairs of thick socks if there is a problem. I want her outfitted for physical training." Quinn almost turned his eyes up to heaven when Doyle stared at him open-mouthed.

"You don't have time for a fit of the giggles." Krista stood before the mirror in the top-floor bathroom of the manor house. She had been given a room in the attic.

"At least it isn't navy-blue passion-killers."

She wore loose-fitting green camouflage trousers, a green T-shirt and a loose green button-up shirt. She'd laced up the black high-top boots that were not too ill-fitting. She wore two pairs of the thick socks she'd been supplied with.

"Time to face the music." She picked up her own clothes and, with these folded over her arm, made her way up one floor to the attic room that would be hers for a while. She'd been ordered to lock the door at all times and not wander where she could get into trouble. "Sounds just like home." She thought briefly of her attic room in the Dumas household.

* * *

"You've had her for ten days now. How is she doing, Sarge?" Captain Waters asked.

The two men stood watching Krista run alone around the track that surrounded the sports field. There were soldiers in the centre doing physical training, being yelled at by their officer.

"Surprised me, Captain." Sergeant Quinn sucked on his moustache. "She can run, has good staying-power, doesn't complain. Got her crawling through muck and the fool woman grins all the way across the field. She don't take no notice of the men heckling her. She'd make a good soldier if she were a man." The highest praise he could give.

"You've had her at the firing range?" Graham Waters had left the training of Krista in Quinn's hands. The man was an expert at turning callow youths into useful soldiers.

"She don't like it much." Quinn sucked in a breath at the foul comments being shouted towards the running woman. He made a mental note of the men. He would be having a word with them – see if he didn't. "But she can break down and reassemble the gun you issued her in the dark. Has a good eye too."

"Time for driving lessons." Waters too had made note of the shouting soldiers. There was no call for shouting such abuse at an innocent female. "I thought Larkin?"

"No, sir, no, not Larkin!" Quinn snapped.

"Why?"

"He don't respect women, sir. I have a girl not much

younger than that one," he jerked his head towards Krista, "and I wouldn't put any female in close quarters with Larkin."

"Thank you." Waters would take the other man's advice. "Who would you suggest? She must learn to drive in all conditions."

"Philpott, sir."

"Philpott … the man flirts with everything in a skirt." Waters stared at his sergeant, shocked.

"He likes women, sir." Quinn said. "No doubt about it but he respects them. The word 'no' means just that to Philpott. Besides, he is hell on wheels, be it riding a motorbike or that sports car of his that roars around the place at all hours."

"I want her trained to handle the large army transport trucks." Waters needed to know if she had the physical strength needed to handle a difficult-to-drive heavy vehicle.

"Philpott is your man, sir." Quinn insisted. He'd have a word in that one's ear before sending him out with young Krista.

"Right." Waters slapped his sergeant's back. "We will add driving lessons to her day. As soon as she is a proficient driver we can get started. Do not let off keeping up the physical training. That too could be vital."

"I don't know what the world is coming to – training women up like a man. I wouldn't want it for any of my own women." Quinn felt comfortable passing remarks with this officer. He wouldn't with all of them.

"If things continue as they are, sergeant – we will all be doing things that we don't like." Waters sighed. The news from the continent was dire.

* * *

"Right." Albus Philpott, Philly to his friends, had been given his orders. "I am going to teach you to drive. Not only that but I will have you changing tyres, checking the oil and putting petrol in her." He patted the side of the large army truck fondly. "By the time I'm finished with you, you'll be able to take this little lady up a glass wall."

"Yes, sir." Krista looked at the huge truck and gulped.

"I am told you have some knowledge of driving?" He wondered what on earth this young woman was doing here. She'd been the talk of the barracks since she arrived. There were a lot of men who had tried to capture her attention. He had thought to try his luck himself but she soon discouraged any ideas of romance. She was always polite but distant.

"I have had what you might call backstreet lessons." Krista didn't want to pretend to know something she didn't. "One of the boys in the family I lived with taught me to drive but I was never allowed out on my own." She thought that covered everything this charming man with his blond hair, blue eyes and flashing smile needed to know.

"Right, jump in and start her up." Philly thanked heavens the truck had one of the new self-starter engines. He couldn't imagine this woman had enough muscle on her to crank up this monster. Although he had noticed she had a nice set of muscles on her. He was only human after all.

Krista climbed up into the truck and wiggled her way into the big seat. She sat for a moment, trying to take in everything around her.

"What's the hold-up?" Philly jumped into the passenger seat and pulled the door closed.

"I need to take a minute to situate myself." Krista refused to be hurried. "This is somewhat different from a car."

"Did anyone ever tell you that you sound like someone off the radio?" Philly was prepared to wait.

"Yes, sir." Krista didn't think he needed to know she had learned to speak English listening to British Broadcasting Corporations language tapes.

The weeks that followed were difficult but fascinating for Krista. She woke early and had breakfast with the people working and living in the manor house. They spoke of the weather or current affairs, but no one spoke of what they were doing in this out-of-the-way spot.

Krista had physical training, weapons training and driving. She drove around the countryside for hours until her arms ached and her legs cramped. She drove through muddy fields, over streams, around obstacles and although not quite a glass wall she did drive over very challenging ground. She spent hours bent over the engine, learning some quick fixes. She could change a tyre and perform basic maintenance on the army truck. She never asked why she needed to know something. If the lesson was offered – she learned.

She collapsed into bed at night exhausted in mind and body. She once more locked her bedroom door and put a chair under the doorknob. She had been aware of the leering looks she received from some of the men. She had ignored them but took precautions.

She wrote to the friends she had made in the

Caulfield household. She could tell them nothing of what she was doing but receiving notes from them kept the loneliness at bay. She was a duck out of water here, surrounded as she was by fighting men.

Chapter 10

"*Perry! What are you doing here?*" Krista had been ordered to present herself at one of the many classroom outbuildings on the land surrounding the manor house.

"*Krista!*" Perry jumped to his feet. "Why are you here and what in heaven's name are you wearing?" He was steady on his feet, thanks to the leather support his father's saddle-maker Gilligan had designed for him.

"The very latest in haute couture," She turned slowly. "It matches your outfit. Do you like it?"

"Sorry to keep you waiting." Captain Waters entered the room, putting an end to any discussion. "Sit down, both of you." He walked to the front of the classroom. The building had been checked for listening devices. One couldn't be too careful. He sat behind the lecturer's desk.

"You have been selected to go on a mission into Germany. You two know each other – are comfortable together – that is important. The mission will be difficult. You will have only each other for back-up and support."

Krista had agreed to go into Germany – for a fee. She had not known that the powers that be intended to send Perry with her. Was she now going to be told what it was Waters wanted of her?

Perry wondered what on earth he signed up for. He had agreed to be trained as an SIS operative. He had been in intensive instruction before being sent off without a word of explanation, ordered to present himself at this classroom.

"You both are almost ready to be sent off on your mission. You have both passed the tests set for you. I did not think you would." Waters had been surprised and pleased by the pair. While they had been challenged mentally and physically, their characters had also been under close scrutiny. They had conducted themselves admirably.

"Can you now tell us what is going on, sir?" Perry said.

"This is the mission you have been selected for – you will travel into Germany to rescue a respected scientist and his wife." Graham Waters was nervous. After all of his careful planning, could they pull this off?

"I beg your pardon?"

Krista was glad Perry had spoken as she was rendered speechless.

"The mission, should you accept it," Waters pinched the bridge of his nose, "will be to travel in a motorised home – a campervan – across the channel into Belgium. The vehicle has been adapted for your use." He picked up the file, pushed his chair back and stood. "Come with me." It would be easier to show them. The vehicle was parked nearby.

They crossed muddy fields to stand staring at the gleaming vehicle that stood out against the green of the field. It was maroon and silver in colour. A vehicle that would attract attention wherever it went.

"Perry, we will want you to exaggerate your injury." Waters opened the door in the side of the vehicle. He stepped inside, waiting for them to follow. He showed them around the home on wheels. Everything that might be needed – kitchen, bathroom, bedroom –was packed neatly into the space. "Krista will drive."

"Sir," Perry had to bend his head to stand in the space, "what exactly do you want from us and more to the point – why us?"

"Take a seat." Waters turned the driver's seat around and locked it in place before sitting. He pointed to the small sofa under a window. "I have been searching for a way to remove people safely from Germany."

"And you believe this is the way?" Perry took a seat beside Krista. He waved around the campervan.

"No, I believe you two are the way," Waters astounded them by saying.

"Perhaps you could explain what you mean by that?" Krista asked.

"My men – the men I would send on this mission – look exactly what they are – well-trained and fit young fighting men. We could try to disguise them, but such things are not always successful."

He waited to see if they had questions, but they just sat across from him and stared – waiting.

"You will present yourselves as a young married

couple from the British upper classes. Perry, you were born to the position. Your accident took you out of those circles, but you know them."

Krista glanced at Perry – she had known that Perry was not your average working Joe.

"Krista, however, needs extensive training on how to appear as one of the many empty-headed debutante beauties that abound in your social circle. I know you understand the kind of women I mean, Perry."

"I do indeed, sir." Perry stared at Krista, wondering if she was capable of appearing to be a social butterfly.

"Captain Caulfield's wife has agreed to help. She has made a list of social occasions you might attend. The clothing needed has been acquired. Lady Winchester's French maid has agreed to groom Krista within an inch of her life. The scene has been set."

"So will I be leaving here, sir?" Krista asked.

"For the moment," Waters said. "Perry will remain here to learn the particulars of the campervan. There have been modifications made that he needs to know about. You, Krista, will be taken to Lady Winchester's home. You must make a study of the young ladies that your hostess will point out to you. Can you do this?"

"I can but try, sir." Krista was confused about the type of person they wanted her to play.

"Nom du chien!" Emmanuelle Doumer, Her Ladyship's maid, stared in true horror at Krista. "What have you been doing – digging ditches?" She threw her hands in the air. "It would be easier to soften leather than your skin – and your hair!" She muttered curses under her breath in French.

94

Krista stood in a bedroom of the Winchester country estate. She was wearing only her undergarments, being examined.

"The clothes I purchased will need to be adjusted," Lia said. "You have changed your body shape."

"Emmanuelle, take her away and do what you can." Abigail Winchester waited until Krista left the room before saying, "Lia, I think it would be a dreadful mistake for Perry to escort Krista to any social functions."

"Why?" Lia and the boys had travelled down to Lia's family home. The boys were in the nursery with their older cousins.

"Krista is a young single girl and should be presented as such. She should not be seen in the company of a male who is not a relative at social occasions." Abigail huffed. "I have been giving thought to the matter." She waited to see if Lia would object before saying, "My eldest daughter Beatrice can introduce Krista to the sort of girls she ought to know. The Duke of Stowe-Grenville's annual ball will be soon enough for Krista to step out in society. I, of course, will be there with my family to see all is as it should be."

"Have you lost the run of your senses, Abigail?" Lia gasped.

Abigail held up her hand and started counting off her fingers. "It will be an ideal location. It will give us time to polish Krista. The ball will be packed with the type of butterflies that we are told she needs to study. It will allow her to speak knowledgably of a stately home if it becomes necessary." She tapped on her thumb. "And finally, finally, she will get a look at the exalted members of her own family."

"Abigail," Lia dropped her head into her hands, "I despair of you!"

"It is ideal," Abigail insisted. "Krista needs time to achieve a polished appearance. What on earth were they thinking of, having her live the life of a soldier and then expecting her to step into the ballroom. It cannot be done, my dear Lia, and you of all people should know that. We have to polish dear Krista until she shines. That will take time."

"I don't think I can do this, Perry." Krista was sitting on one side of the table they had unpacked and put in the centre of the van. She had been picked up that morning by an army driver and delivered to the manor. She spent the morning learning to drive the vehicle and discovering the mysteries of its interior.

"What – drive this beast?" Perry was sitting in the driver's seat turned to face Krista.

"No!" she waved her hand dismissively. "That is a doddle after the army truck. I mean, appear to be silly." She had been introduced to more giggling young girls then she would have believed existed – *on the entire planet!*

"You must find a character that fits you." Perry had been receiving a great deal of instruction in covert action. Who would have believed his injury could prove to be a blessing? The men in charge appeared to believe that, because of it, he would be underestimated in the field. With the new leather brace, he was almost back to his old self.

"Perry, I have had afternoon tea, coffee mornings and visits to the modiste with a gaggle of giggling girls.

They insist on shouting at me as if being French renders me deaf!" She almost wailed. "I cannot give the appearance of being that young and silly. I simply cannot!"

"You certainly look the part," He threw his hands up in front of him when she glared. "I am a man. I cannot help but notice."

"I have been primped, powdered, pummelled until I want to scream. I have been soaked in so much oil I am afraid of striking a match in case I turn into a burning inferno." She dropped her head onto her arms on top of the table. "What am I going to do, Perry?"

"Make a pot of tea?" He could not allow her to sink into despair.

"I beg your pardon?" She raised her head to send him a murderous glance.

"The interior of this," he waved a hand around the van, "will be your responsibility. I have learned to pack and unpack every item. You must learn to reach for items without searching. There is a spirit burner and kettle in there." He pointed to one of the fitted cupboards.

"Perry, how am I going to learn to act silly?" She searched the cupboards, making mental note of the location of each item. She took the little spirit burner and its three-legged metal stand out and put it on the marble shelf that fit into the space between top and bottom of the fitted cupboard. She removed two heavy porcelain mugs. She was astonished to note the tiny oven attached to the marble shelf. What a clever little van it was, she thought, patting it fondly. Why, it even had a sink and running water!

"Listen, my darling . . ." He laughed when she shot him a glance over her shoulder. "Hey, we are supposed to be married. I can hardly call you Krista and Frenchy doesn't seem appropriate."

"You are very cheerful." She filled the small kettle, marvelling once more at the clever design of the vehicle.

"Krista —"

She turned to give him her full attention. He sounded so serious.

"I thought this," he hit his leg, "had turned me into a useless article doomed to sit back and watch life pass me by ..."

She put the kettle on top of the little spirit burner and waited.

"What we are doing — removing someone from under Hitler's nose — it has given new meaning to my life. I want us to succeed."

She stood with her back to him, keeping her eye on the spirit burner and kettle. It looked unsteady to her. "Perry, what if I can't do it? I have tried and tried in the privacy of my bedroom to act like the girls I have met act — it is simply not possible for me to be convincing. I look and sound insane!"

"I'm sorry." Perry didn't know what to say. "Have you met no one you could admire?"

"There is Hermione who giggles in a way that injures the ears. Beatrice who can discuss gown trimmings until my head aches. They can all talk for hours — about nothing at all!" There were tears in her eyes when she looked at him. She did not want to fail. "How can I act in such a fashion?"

"Perhaps you should make up a story about yourself that works for you." He leaned over to take her hand. "You don't have to be a copy of anyone. If you believe in the image you portray – so will others."

Krista stared at him. Wasn't that what she had been doing ever since she arrived in England? She was no longer Krista Dumas, the serving girl from the *auberge du ville*, she was – who was she?

"I will ask Lia for help."

Krista had been struggling. She had help close to hand. Lia Caulfield and Lady Winchester were not giggling women. They had both taken their destiny into their own hands. She would approach them this very evening for help. Lia was driving down with the boys for the weekend. Violet too would be joining them. She could not imagine Violet had ever giggled inanely.

"I will work very hard at presenting the image of a girl you would marry."

"Steady on, old thing!" Perry was glad to see her improved humour. "I consider myself far too young to marry!"

They settled down to enjoy their tea and discuss their upcoming journey. There were a great many practical matters that needed to be handled and both needed to learn their way around what they were both calling 'the van'. This occupied their time until the car arrived to take Krista back to the Winchester estate.

"*Bravo, bravo!*" The sound of clapping hands echoed around the red drawing room.

"It works?" Krista stared at Abigail, Violet and Lia, her heart in her mouth. She had just enacted the character she had developed for their opinion.

"Far better than being a complete flibbertigibbet!" Violet said.

"The silly young goose they wanted you to portray would not dream of driving across Europe and camping in a muddy field – men!" Abigail huffed.

"Am I wrong to feel flattered?" Lia smiled. "I thought I recognised actions of my own in your character."

"I modelled myself on you, Lia, and other ladies from your exercise class." Krista wanted to fall on the floor. She had worked hard to find a character that would not feel completely alien to her. "I thought the women I have met while in your company would be the sort of women who could drive a large vehicle and walk grandly across muddy fields in wellington boots."

"Quite right, my dear." Abigail beamed. "We have Saturday evening and the ball to get through and then you and Perry can be off on your adventure." She wasn't sure how she should feel about a young unmarried couple being in such close quarters with each other.

"The ball," Krista sat down heavily. "I feel as if I have accomplished one task and before I can take a deep breath it is time for another."

"You consider going to a ball a task?" Abigail laughed. "My dear, there are thousands that would envy you."

"I will look forward to hearing all about it." Violet was not of the social class that attended ducal balls.

"Abagail and I will be there to help you through every stage," Lia promised.

"Wonderful." Krista tried not to grimace. Could any of these women really understand what a strange new world all of this was to her?

Ah well, she had made the choice to chart her own

course in life. She couldn't start to complain now. She was as ready as she would ever be. It would not be the fault of these women if she failed.

She gulped air and looked around the room at the smiling faces – she could do this – she could.

To Be Continued

Printed in Great Britain
by Amazon